I0746268

THE BOX

THE BOX
A MECANA STORY

John L. Lansdale

BookVoice Publishing 2019

This novel is a work of fiction. All incidents and all characters are fictionalized, with the exception that well-known historical and public figures are products of the author's imagination and are not to be construed as real. Where real-life historical figures appear, the situations and dialogues concerning those persons are fictional and are not intended to depict actual events within the fictional confines of the story. In all other respects, any resemblance to persons living or dead is entirely coincidental.

ISBN
978-1-949381-10-8 Paperback
978-1-949381-11-5 eBook

BookVoice Publishing
PO Box 1528
Chandler, TX 75758
www.bookvoicepublishing.com

<u>**THE MECANA SERIES by John L. Lansdale**</u>
#1 - Horse of a Different Color
#2 - When the Night Bird Sings
#3 - Twisted Justice
#4 – The Box

<u>**OTHER WORKS BY JOHN L. LANSDALE**</u>
Slow Bullet
Long Walk Home
Zombie Gold
The Last Good Day
Broken Moon
Shadows West (with Joe R. Lansdale)
Hell's Bounty (with Joe R. Lansdale)
Boy and Hog (Short Story)
Boy and Hog Return (Short Story)
Emergency Christmas (Short Story)
Tales from the Crypt (Comic Series)
That Hellbound Train (Graphic Novel)
Yours Truly, Jack the Ripper (Graphic Novel)
Shadow Warrior (Graphic Novel)
Justin Case (Graphic Novel)

What Others are Saying about John L. Lansdale

"Mickey Spillane fans will welcome this page-turner...Lansdale effectively delays revealing the novel's big secret until the end. Those who like their thrillers with a heavy dose of violent action will be satisfied." - *Publishers Weekly* review of **Slow Bullet**

"This is an entertaining, science fiction-historical-horror blend with resourceful protagonists and a solid cast of secondary characters."
- *Booklist* review of **Zombie Gold**

"**Slow Bullet** is a straight-ahead thriller...it's about action, and there's plenty of that. Check it out." - *Bill Crider's Pop Culture Magazine*

"...the author's innate ability to spin a complex tale painted with vivid characters and intense suspense provides readers with a well-paced book that they may find difficult to set down...a worthwhile suspenseful ride." - *Amazing Stories* review of **Horse of a Different Color**

"Has something for everyone... It's exciting, entertaining and educational. A fun ride." – legendary TV personality/actress/author Joan Hallmark, review of **Zombie Gold**

"...something unique and comfortable and difficult to put down. Highly recommended." – *Cemetery Dance* review of **Hell's Bounty**

"True to Lansdale tradition, John L. Lansdale has compiled a piece of work that should appeal to a wide range of readers."
– *Amazing Stories* review of **Zombie Gold**

"**Long Walk Home** really touched and gripped me. A great bittersweet story of light and shadow about growing up in a time gone by. I loved it." – Joe R. Lansdale

For hardcore horror fans.

Chapter 1

On a dead-end street, a man barricaded himself in his house, holding his wife and two children hostage. Outside the house, Thomas Mecana and Darcie Connors are hunkered down in the street, on the other side of Mecana's truck, guns in their hands.

"How long did the police say it would take to get here?" Mecana asked Darcie.

"They didn't say," she said.

"This needs someone better trained for it than we are," Mecana said. "You did tell the cops who and where we are, didn't you?"

"Yes, one of the cops is Nelson."

"Just in case, when they get here, let them see us lay the guns down."

The barricaded man bolted out the front door, wild-eyed and carrying an automatic rifle, blowing even more holes in Mecana's truck. Ammo magazines were sticking out of both front pockets of his black pinstriped suit, his coat sleeves ripped under his arms and a purple tie pulled down on his white shirt. The tie and his bushy black hair were blowing in the wind as he ran across the street. He looked like a spider with his long legs churning and waving his arms around in all directions.

"Shit, I got to go get him," Mecana said.

"Let the cops get him," Darcie said.

"He might kill someone if I don't."

"Yeah it could be you."

"Check on the hostages." Mecana jumped up, cut across the street and began a foot race.

The man stopped and turned to fire at Mecana as he ducked behind a nearby car. The man peppered the car with bullets and took off again, running across a lawn, headed for the front door of a neighbor's house. Mecana turned on the speed and caught the man as he reached for the doorknob, knocking him down, his weapon flying out of his hands, sliding across the porch and falling off the edge to the ground.

Mecana reached to the back of his belt, drew his Glock and pointed it at him. "Stay down," he said. "I don't want to kill you."

"But that's what I want you to do."

The man jumped to his feet. Mecana pitched his Glock out on the lawn. He tackled the man and wrestled him down, rolling him on his stomach. He grabbed the man's arms and pulled them behind his back. Cops came running up.

"Who's who?" one of the cops asked.

"That's Mecana holding the suspect, don't shoot," Nelson said. He yanked the handcuffs off his belt and snapped them on the man.

Mecana leaned up against the front door huffing and puffing as Nelson pulled the shooter to his feet and another cop grabbed the cuffs on the man's wrist and walked him to the patrol car. Suddenly, the front door came open and Mecana fell down with it. A big, bearded man wearing a Dallas Cowboys shirt and cap stepped out pointing a double-barrel shotgun under Mecana's chin.

"What the hell is going on?"

"I had to bring down a shooter," Mecana said. "Everything's alright now."

"You a cop?"

"No, but he is." Mecana pointed at the uniformed Sergeant Nelson.

"Put that shotgun down," Nelson said.

The homeowner looked out on his lawn at all the cops and laid the shotgun down on the porch. Another cop picked it up.

"Are the woman and kids alright?" Mecana asked, standing up.

"Yeah, Darcie's with them now," Nelson said. "An ambulance is going to take them to the hospital just to make sure."

"You got here just in time," Mecana said. "I'm getting too old for this kind of shit."

"I noticed that."

Mecana eyed Nelson's stern look, retrieved his Glock and holstered it.

A television news van pulled up across the street. A reporter holding her microphone and a cameraman began setting up outside it. They filmed the cop putting the shooter away in the car and some other footage from the street.

Nelson told the big guy to go back inside his house – without the shotgun – and he did.

Nelson walked across the street and confronted the TV crew.

"It's all over," he said. "You can get more info at the station than here."

The reporter nodded and they got back in the van and left.

Nelson walked back across the street to Mecana.

"Man, they sure come out of the woodwork." he said, shaking his head. "How the hell did you and Darcie even get into this mess, Mecana?"

"Bad timing, I guess," Mecana said. "Got a call from a woman wanting to talk to us about a divorce, said her husband was running around on her. Asked us to come to her house. We pulled up in the drive and that nut drove up behind us. Had us blocked in when he started to open fire and ran in the house."

"Trouble follows you around," Nelson said.

"Looks that way."

"Anyways, thanks for your help," Nelson said with a grin. They were shaking hands when Darcie walked up. "You may be a widow if Mecana keeps chasing bad guys."

"Yeah, looks like I'm going to have to take out a bigger life insurance policy on him," she said.

"Good thinking. Take care, you two," Nelson said and headed for his cruiser.

Darcie turned to Mecana, "Want to see if your truck will start?"

"It just might." Mecana brushed himself off and they walked toward the truck. "It should at least get us home."

"And if it doesn't?"

"We'll do what we always do: call DeMax."

"The insurance company may not insure another of these," Darcie said as they got into the truck.

"We'll talk about that later."

The truck cranked on the third try and Mecana and Darcie drove off.

A few minutes later, Darcie broke the silence. "That was Cindy's husband Chris Summerfield they hauled in," she said. "They've been married fifteen years. He owned an apparel business that was doing pretty well. At least his wife and kids weren't harmed. Well, physically, at least. Emotionally...that'll take a while. It all started when he called her and she told him everything. That we were on our way to the house, that she was leaving him and going to get everything he had because he had been cheating on her. That's what set him off."

"I can see why," Mecana said. "The house alone is worth a million, easy. He's apparently got a lot of money at stake in a divorce."

"He should have kept his dick in his pants."

"We don't know for sure he was cheating on her," Mecana said. "We were still looking into it."

"Yeah, probably nothing serious," Darcie rolled her eyes. "I bet he just wanted a little strange, some of that recreational pussy."

Mecana twisted his head like a bulldog, trying to figure out where that came from.

"Whatever," he said. "She doesn't need us anymore now. Besides, I could use a little recreation myself, relieve some of that tension from wrestling with numb-nuts."

"When you get you another truck, check on a new car for me," Darcie said, ignoring the last comment. "Got almost a hundred-thousand miles on mine."

Mecana didn't say anything, just turned his truck onto a side street as smoke bellowed out from under the hood.

"You need an interpreter?" Darcie said.

"No, I get your message. Loud and clear."

Darcie smiled and leaned back in her seat. Mecana turned to her with a grin and she looked at him, still smiling. They both broke into a laugh.

"What kind of ride do you want?" Mecana said, a slight chuckle jumping out.

"What kind do you want?" Darcie said and winked.

The truck's engine kept coughing black smoke out as they drove.

"We may have to call DeMax," Darcie said.

"Hope not."

But, after barely making it home in the limping truck, Mecana called DeMax after all.

"Wanted to give you the news before it comes on TV," Mecana said. "Me and Darcie are okay but some nutso tried to kill us. I got my truck shot up...again. I need you to take me to look for another one."

"Again?" DeMax said. "That's, what, three? What the hell happened?"

"I just told you," Mecana said.

"You're sure going to have a hell of a time getting insurance now."

"I know. Already heard about that, too. So, can you take me to the lot?"

"Sure," DeMax said. "No problem."

Darcie was standing by Mecana, listening in.

"Tell him to bring Mabre, too. She can keep me company while you two go look for your new truck and my tricked out red Bullitt Mustang."

"I'll tell her to get ready," DeMax said. "See you two in about an hour."

Mecana hung up the phone. "Damn, I may have to buy a used truck."

"You don't have to buy me anything if we can't afford it," Darcie said.

"Yes I do. I know when to say calf rope."

"What's that mean?"

"What my daddy used to say. Means you're hog tied."

"And…what's that mean?"

Mecana shook his head. "Means I've got to buy you a new car. First, I need to call Emily and see when she's coming for her visit."

"Can't wait for her to visit, I've got some great plans for us," Darcie said. "We're going to have a really good time."

"That sounds like it's going to cost me too."

"Oh, it definitely will," Darcie said and smiled. "I can keep the car I've got and —"

"No, no," Mecana said, interrupting. "Let's not talk about it anymore. I'll just have the insurance company send a claims adjuster to look at the truck."

"They'll go berserk once they get the report," Darcie said.

"Not my fault."

"They're going to think so. You kind of have a history with this kind of stuff."

"Just goes with the territory. We're in a dangerous business, after all."

"They won't care."

"Hey! Whose side are you on, anyways?"

"The side with reality."

"Can't argue with that," Mecana said.

Chapter 2

Mecana paid cash for a used truck with a basic liability insurance policy. He financed Darcie's tricked-out red Mustang with a full coverage policy. Mecana and DeMax drove the vehicles back to Mecana's house.

That night, they all went out to Brogans for dinner. DeMax was kind enough to let Darcie drive him in her new Mustang. The owner of Brogans wasn't too happy to see DeMax. He didn't say anything, just kept eyeing DeMax and putting his hand in his pocket, like he might have a gun and could blow DeMax's head off at any minute.

DeMax just smiled at him and only opened his mouth to eat. It was obvious he didn't want his new bride to know about his past encounters with the restaurant owner's wife.

While they ate, Mabre and Darcie planned a get-together to entertain Mecana's daughter Emily when she arrived, and Demax and Mecana watched a baseball game on the wall TV.

After parting ways in the parking lot, Darcie took a long drive across town to break in her new Mustang, telling Mecana how much she liked the old Bullitt movie with Steve McQueen, and about how all the chase scenes with the Mustang is why she's always wanted one.

Mecana was planning on how she would pay for it, one way or another. It would probably be another, he figured, as she gunned the Mustang like McQueen did in the movie.

The next morning, after a late night and an early breakfast, Mecana got a call from Dallas Homicide Detective Sunday Verves.

"I saw what happened yesterday," Sunday said. "Are you and Darcie okay?"

"Yeah, we're fine."

"Good. Got a question for you"

"What is it?"

"Something is missing from the property room. Thought maybe you could help us with it."

"Not sure if I could help you," Mecana said. "I've been retired for several years now. What are you looking for, drugs?"

"That and the evidence box you left in the property room. The one from the Durant case – 'The Mutilator' case. You know anything about the box we don't?"

"I doubt it," Mecana said. "Scene pictures, coroner and autopsy report, and all that was left in a folder in the chief's office. The only items in the box were what we found in Lisa's mansion. Mostly stuff from the 1800s. An old Gladstone bag and some gruesome murder paraphernalia from that time period, I think."

"That's interesting," Sunday said. "We discovered the drugs and evidence box missing when one of the officers noticed a glob of wet toilet paper on the property room camera lens. Had to be that day or the toilet paper wouldn't have still been wet."

"That was a good observation," Mecana said.

"Whoever it was stole the Mutilator evidence and over two hundred grand worth of cocaine. Our evidence officer Dewey Flanagan was off that day. Said he lost his key the day before. But if he did, and someone found it, how would anyone know what it unlocked? And what did the evidence box have to do with the cocaine?"

"Might have just put the drugs in the box to make it easier to carry. Taking the bag was probably coincidental. Unless it was someone who knew what that particular box was."

"We felt kind of stupid for letting it happen," Sunday said. "I need you to fill out some forms for our records, in case any of the evidence shows back up. I can drop them off at your office today. I'll be in that area anyway."

"We closed the office down after Knight-Bird-Candy Kane fiasco went down. We're working out of the house now," Mecana said. "We put an ad in the newspaper and on the net. Doing better with that for less money and save a lot more gas and time. Only thing I have left from the office is the front door. Had 'Connors and Mecana – Private Investigators' painted on it. I hung it in the bathroom as a joke, but Darcie liked it so much we kept it."

"That's amusing. I bet Darcie was surprised."

"To say the least. I'll come by the station and get the form."

"Okay, tell Darcie I said hi and bye."

Mecana hung up the phone as Darcie walked in the room.

"Who was that? I heard you say something about a box."

"It was Sunday," Mecana said. "That evidence box from the Durant case is missing from the property room. Sunday wants me to fill out a form describing all the contents."

"The Mutilator case? But that would defeat the whole reason we didn't tell anyone what was in there in the first place."

"Maybe we overreacted," Mecana said. "Looking back, I don't think anyone would catch on to what we think we know, or link it to where we found the bag. It's disassociated from all that."

"What could have happened?"

"No telling."

"If someone took it, why would they want it?" Darcie said. "You think they're looking to harm someone?"

"You never know."

"You remember what was in the bag?" Darcie said. "I didn't even get a good look."

"I don't think I'll ever forget it."

Chapter 3

Mecana drove to the station, memories of the Durant case rushing through his mind. He hoped to hell something like that never happened again. He parked in the parking lot that had doubled the price since he had last been there. He shook his head. "One of these days, we're going to have to pay for the air we breathe," he said to the blinking ticket vending machine.

Across the street and up in the Homicide Department, a tall, good-looking officer by the name of Eddy Hanson was pouring himself a cup of coffee when Mecana walked through the door.

Eddy offered Mecana a cup but he shook his head no, thinking of Verve's bad coffee.

"What are you doing here, Mecana?"

"I need to speak with Sunday. Speaking of, you two married yet?"

"We've been dating. Nothing serious yet. I'm trying to make it that way."

"I can understand why," Mecana said. "She's a beautiful, smart woman."

"Yeah, I'm a lucky man."

Sunday walked in the office and saw Mecana and Eddy talking. She was wearing jeans on her curvy body, a dark forest-green shirt with rhinestone buttons, her police badge pinned on her belt beside her automatic. Her black eyes sparkling, long black hair bouncing on her shoulders with every step.

"Hey Mecana," she said. "You caught me at a bad time."

"Anytime with you is a good time," Mecana said and smiled. Sunday hugged his neck.

"I'll have to remember that one, Mecana," Eddy said.

"I'll get the paperwork for you." Sunday walked over to her desk and picked up the form, handing it to Mecana. "You can fill it out and I'll put it on file."

"What was Dewey's story?" Mecana asked.

"Dewey was off that day, and since we're understaffed, there was no one in the property room."

"He said he lost his key. That's a little hard to believe."

"We questioned everyone on the property log that signed in and out for evidence but no luck," Sunday said.

"People are always taking a short cut out the exit in there. Just not sure who did on that day."

"I noticed it was there several times before I left the department," Mecana said. "The Durant case was the most horrific case I have ever worked, and that box had a bag full of murder tools."

"If you want to help find it, I can appoint you as a temporary investigator for lost police property, if the chief will let me," Sunday said. "You know Walt, don't you?"

"Yeah, good cop, deserves his promotion," Mecana said. "Doubt we need to take it that far, though."

"Not a big deal since we wont have a trial," Sunday said. "We don't need it anymore, except for accountability purposes. Unless it's connected to another murder."

"Darcie and I have a meeting with a client this afternoon. Let me think on it and I'll get the form back to you."

"No problem. Nice to see you again," Sunday said. "Tell Darcie we need to get together soon."

"I will, say hi to your mom and dad for me."

They both walked away. Mecana took a quick look around the office for old time's sake. He saw the new homicide chief Walter Harris on the phone in his glassed-in office. He was always watching his weight and still looked fit. He had a little less hair than when he was working the street and picked up some wrinkles over the last twenty years. He had a pretty wife in the medical field, Mecana remembered, and his two girls had to be almost grown. It looked like Sunday might be in line for chief when Harris retired. Mecana thought that would make Sunday's dad proud, having his daughter hold the same position he once did.

Mecana could still see Robert Verves sitting in the office, and remembered the difficult times they had with the

Durant case. How pressured everyone was to solve it or get fired.

Mecana called Darcie on the way home and filled her in on what happened at the station.

"Are we going to look for it?" Darcie said.

"I don't know. Emily is going to come to see us soon I want to be with her. May run down to Austin one weekend to see Morgan, too."

"Me and Mabre are going to keep Emily busy."

"That's a sweet thing to do. I have to figure out what I'm going to do to make her happy with me."

"Just be yourself and she'll be happy," Darcie said. "Worked on me."

"You're sure being nice."

"I plan on being the same way when you get home."

Mecana perked up. Finding the box was suddenly not as important as it was five minutes ago. Darcie and the kids were much more important than whatever happened to the box. It was probably all insignificant, anyway, he thought, and picked up speed.

Chapter 4

Friday evening at the Eagle's Nest apartment building, seventh floor, a middle-aged man with a rugged-looking face was standing at the door of apartment 709. He was clean-shaven, wearing a red cap and a lightweight tan jacket, holding a nondescript package under his left arm. His right hand was in his jacket pocket and his gloved left index finger under the package was pushing the doorbell. His face was partly covered by his upturned jacket collar.

A woman's voice could be heard from behind the door. "Who is it?"

"Are you Mary Nichols?" the man said through the door.

"Yes. What do you want?"

"I have a package for you."

"From who?"

"Baytown Pharmaceutical."

"That's my employer," she said. "What on earth could it be."

"You have to sign for it," the man said. "It's Friday night, lady, and I don't work on weekends. Open the door."

"No. Go away."

"I'll hand a pen and the form to you, sign it and hand it back to me. I'll leave the package at the door and go away."

He shifted his weight, took another grip on the package and looked around the empty hallway again.

The woman cracked open the door and noticed the package under his arm. She reached through the gap for the pen.

He took another quick glance at the empty hall and threw his weight against the door, knocking it open and causing her to stumble backwards and fall to the floor. He pitched the package inside and slammed the door behind him. Dropping to the floor, he cupped his hand over her mouth and rolled her over on her stomach, Out of his jacket pocket came a rope which he looped around her neck, pulling the rope as tight as he could, cutting off her air until she was limp on the floor. He turned the rope loose, stood up and opened the package on the floor. Inside sat an old, black leather Gladstone bag.

He took off his jacket and swiped a hand across the dining room table, knocking off a candle holder and dishes, and placed the young woman on the table with her legs hanging off. He opened the bag, removed a long knife and cut her throat from ear to ear. Blood gushed out, matting in her long brown hair as it ran across the table down to the floor.

He removed a railroad spike and a tack hammer from the bag and drove the spike into her ear with the hammer, deep into her brain.

He wiped the blood of his knife blade across the laced collar of Mary's blue dress and placed the knife back on the table beside the hammer, leaving the spike in her ear.

He rolled up her dress to her waist and ripped off her silk panties, put on a rubber and spread her legs. He shot his wad in less than a minute. He left the condom on and zipped his pants

He took sneakers and pants out of the bag and put the knife and hammer back in. He then spent several minutes taking off his bloody clothes and shoes and putting on fresh ones from the bag, which he replaced with the bloody clothes. He sat the bag back in the package and picked it up, holding it snug against his side to prevent it from falling apart. He opened the door and peeked out. Still empty. He stepped out into the hallway and closed the door behind him.

He stepped into the elevator, turned up the collar of his jacket and rode down to the bottom floor. Twelve minutes after his arrival, the man was exiting the building through revolving doors.

He walked half a block down the street to a bus stop, sat down on a bench with the package under his arm, watching people walk by, smiling at the ones who looked his way every now and then.

The bus drove on for miles. When he finally stepped off, he walked over to a Cadillac Escalade parked across the street, unlocked the door, got in and sat the package in the passenger seat. He started the car and drove away.

Twenty minutes later he arrived at his three-bedroom house, sitting on a hill separated from his neighbors by three acres. He parked in the garage and went inside the house, package under his arm.

A big yellow cat ran up to him. He sat the package down in the kitchen and fed the cat, grabbing a beer from the refrigerator for himself and drank it down. He unrolled a trash bag, dropped the bottle in, and carried the trash bag and package to the bathroom, sitting them on the floor. He took the leather Gladstone bag out of the package and sat it on the sink. Then he unzipped his pants, took the rubber off, pitched it in the commode and flushed.

He looked at himself in the mirror.

"I didn't pick you…your name picked me." He said to the Dallas/Fort Worth phone book lying by the sink.

The man removed his clothes and shoes and tossed them in with the other clothes. He reached up to his face and began peeling off a plastic-looking film. When it was gone, he looked years younger. His complexion was smoother and younger, even his nose appeared smaller.

He turned the shower on, stepped in and began scrubbing his body with a hard bristled brush until his skin began to bleed. He turned the water off and stepped out to dry himself off, leaving streaks of blood behind on the towel. He pulled on the sink and the entire fixture separated from the wall, showing a small hole in the wall. He placed the leather bag in the opening and pushed the sink back in place.

He picked up the trash bag and his phone and carried them to his bedroom naked. He put the trash bag under the bed then sat down to check his voicemail.

"I'll be back in town tomorrow," a woman's voice said. "I'll call you when I get home."

That was it.

He laid his phone on an end table, turned the lamp off and pulled a sheet over the lower part of his naked body. The cat jumped on the bed and curled up at his feet.

Chapter 5

It was Monday morning before Mary was found. Her friend and coworker Judy came by to take her to work. When she didn't answer, Judy opened the door with her key and went inside. She saw Mary on the dining room table, covered in blood with her dress pulled up, showing her naked body from the waist down. Her legs were hanging off the table. Judy screamed and ran out of the apartment, tripping over her own feet and falling to her knees in the hallway.

Several of Mary's neighbors appeared at their doors and saw Judy on the floor. A middle-aged lady wearing a pink robe with curlers in her hair ran out of her apartment to Judy.

"What happened?" the lady asked.

Judy pointed toward the open door with a shaky hand. "My friend is in there covered in blood!"

A man in pajamas was standing in his doorway, watching, and said, "I'll call the police."

The elderly lady nodded and put her arms around Judy, still on the floor with tears and mascara streaming down her face, dotting her bright red dress.

Two other men appeared from their apartments and went in Mary's apartment for a look. They were both back out in a flash.

"She's dead," one of them said. "It's horrible. She's been mutilated."

"I think I'm going to throw up," the other man said.

The man who called the police came back to the door and told Judy they were on the way. Judy was still on the floor, leaning against the wall.

Once the security guard arrived he closed Mary's apartment door and stood guard, waiting for the police.

Thirty minutes later the police arrived. Sunday and Eddy showed up. The forensic squad took pictures and searched for evidence. Medics gave Judy tranquilizers, bandaged her knees and Sunday let her go home with a request to have another talk after she had time to recuperate from the horrible experience. Sunday notified Mary's family and asked them to meet her at the morgue to identify the body.

No details of the murder were released to the press but reporters still gathered in a restricted area for details. Sunday promised them more information once the coroner released his report.

Eddy walked up to Sunday, shaking his head. "The coroner said she's been dead for two or three days."

"We'll know if we got a suspect when we get the camera footage from the Eagle's Nest," Sunday said. "Don't answer any questions from the press."

"I won't. This looks like what Mecana and Darcie were dealing with on the Durant case."

"Now we've got our own," Sunday said. "Put Mary Nichols' and Judy Weller's info in the database and see what we have."

Eddy nodded and walked away.

Forensic Detective Barry Cannon walked up to Sunday.

"Barry, take a good look at the spike. It looks like there might be some numbers under all that rust."

"That's chilling. Glad the coroner has to remove it."

"Yeah the horror of it is devastating."

"I'll look in to it and get back to you as soon as I can," Barry said and walked away.

Sunday was still searching the apartment for evidence when the new Homicide Chief – Walter Harris, a man who had waited his turn for twenty years – phoned her from his office.

"Did you know your case is on TV already?"

"No. I barred the press from coming in until we got everything done," Sunday said. "I told them there would be a press conference later."

"Well they didn't listen."

"What made it on?"

"First they had video of the victim being wheeled out of the building in a bag," Harris said, "then they interviewed some residents from the building. A reporter even said the victim had been mutilated and raped. How did they know that?"

"I don't know," Sunday said. "We damn sure didn't tell them. She was mutilated, though, and raped."

"Shut it down, now. Lock the apartment and put a guard on it. I'll go with you to see her family at the morgue. Call and tell them."

"Already have," Sunday said. "Meet you there at two."

"We'll crank it up again tomorrow without the press knowing," Harris said and hung up.

Chapter 6

Mecana was putting his Marine Corps shirt and basketball shorts in his workout bag when Darcie came in and turned on the bedroom TV.

"Look at this," she said. "Somebody murdered a woman at the Eagle's Nest. They're saying she was mutilated and raped. Her name was Mary Nichols and she's been dead for several days."

"Something about that name sounds familiar to me but I don't know why," Mecana said.

"You claim everything sounds familiar to you."

"That's because I have a memory like a steel trap."

"Or one who thinks he does."

Mecana rolled his eyes. "You ready to go to the gym?"

"I don't know, are you going to yell 'Gung Ho' when we start working out as usual?"

"Of course."

"Figured you would," Darcie said.

They picked up their gym bags and walked out of the house and into the Mustang.

"Think I'll call Sunday," Mecana said. "See what she can tell us." He dialed her number as Darcie drove away.

Sunday answered. "Hey Mecana. Don't tell me, you saw what happened on TV."

"Yep," Mecana said, putting her on speakerphone. "Is it true what they were saying?"

"Yes, and a whole lot more."

"Who gave your case away?" Mecana asked.

"No idea," Sunday said. "Walt told us to shut it down until we met with the family and the press backs off. We'll probably get going again tomorrow. Looks like a sex killing. Nothing missing from her purse or apartment and no signs of a struggle, other than a few scratches on the floor. Signs point to a surprise attack. Could've been someone she knew. Found some bloody footprints that may help. Not supposed to tell you this, but I know I can trust you: She was strangled. Her throat was slit. She was raped. And a railroad spike was driven through her ear into her brain."

Mecana and Darcie gasped.

"That is horrible," Darcie said.

"Familiar, too," Mecana said.

"How so?" Sunday asked.

"A railroad spike went missing with the stolen evidence box. It was in the leather bag," Mecana said. "That very spike was used the same way a long time ago in Austin. I never told anyone about it being in the bag, except Darcie."

"I'm having Barry take a good look at it now," Sunday said.

"If it's the same as the one in the box, there should be blood stains and UP1436 imprinted on it, for Union Pacific Railroad," Mecana said. "A number that's been embedded into my brain."

"I thought it was rust," Sunday said, trailing off.

"Sounds like it might be the same one from the bag," Mecana said. "There's a lot more we need to speak about, in person."

"Think it is. I'll get back to you soon," Sunday said.

Mecana hung up and looked at Darcie.

"The killer must have found out how the spike was used and did a copycat murder."

"Heaven forbid," Darcie said. "It's coming back to haunt us."

Chapter 7

It was a little after midnight on Ranch Street, four days after Mary Nichols was murdered. Under flashing neon lights advertising an adult movie theater, a skinny young kid was sitting on the sidewalk beside the theater door, playing saxophone, an upturned cap on the pavement to collect coins and the occasional dollar bill.

A half block down the street, a blonde white girl and a black girl were standing on the corner, applying their trade, watching cars pull up and making deals.

A gray sedan pulled up to the curb beside the black girl and let the window down. She walked to the car and leaned in the passenger window. "Want to party?"

"Don't that seem obvious," the man in the car said, staring at her breasts resting on the car windowsill.

The man tugged the bill of his black cap tighter on his head and started moving his gloved hands loosely around on the steering wheel, like he might speed away at any moment. He leaned over toward the window and held up five hundred-dollar bills.

The blonde saw the money and walked up to the car, too. She could see part of his face behind the other girl.

"How about two?" the blonde said.

"Nope, three's a crowd," he said.

The blonde flipped him off and walked back to the corner.

He held up the money again and waved it at the remaining girl. She snatched at the money and he drew it away from her.

"Get in and I'll give it to you," he said.

She opened the door and got inside when she noticed a black leather bag in the back seat, sitting on folded coveralls, and decided to keep her hand on the door handle.

"No rough stuff," she said. "If you got something weird in that bag, deal's off."

"Just want a good fucking, Annie."

She froze for a moment. "How do you know my name?" she asked. "Are you a cop or something?"

"Could be," he said. "They call you Annie Sweets, but it's really Annie Chapman, right?"

"You must be a cop," she said. "What, you going to arrest me now?"

"Nope. I'll still give you the five hundred for the rest of the night. We got a deal or not?"

Annie scooted over on the seat and closed the door. "Give me the cash."

He handed her the money, put the car in gear and drove away.

"Go to the Ritz hotel," Annie said, counting the money.

"No need to do that, we'll use the back seat. I'll find a place to park."

"Cheapskate."

"You got paid, what's it matter?" He turned into an alley next to Suzy's Cafe and drove to a dark spot shaded from the moon by buildings.

"Okay, over you go. I'll get this out of your way." He reached over his seat for the bag and coveralls.

She reached over to his crotch and rubbed his pants. "Get that thing up," she said and rubbed again. "I don't feel nothing."

"You will."

"I'll let you know when you get your five hundred worth." Annie dropped her shorts and panties as she climbed over the front seat into the back seat. "Let's get this over with."

He opened the bag and reached his hand in.

The car rocked and a muffled scream jumped out of the car with no one to hear it. Less than ten minutes later, he stepped out of the front passenger door wearing city sanitation coveralls, carrying the black bag, and hurriedly walked away to the opposite street.

Three women walked past the restaurant without so much as a glance at the car in the alley, windows fogged up from the early morning air.

Chapter 8

Next morning as daylight crept into the alley over the tall buildings, a frail young man wearing an usher uniform and carrying a lunchbox was walking through the alley to work when he saw the parked sedan. He walked up to the car and yelled, "Anyone in there!?"

He tapped on the window. No answer.

"Going to be garbage trucks coming through here in the next hour or so," he said to whoever was in the car. "They'll run right over you."

Still no answer.

He pulled on all the locked doors with larceny in mind, cupped his hands over his eyes and stuck his face against a back door window. He squinted his eyes and looked in. He jumped back and dropped his lunch box, then stepped back up to the window and looked in again.

"Oh my god." He left his lunchbox on the ground and limped to Suzy's Café around the corner.

He found a stool inside. Two stools nearby were occupied by skinny young prostitutes – one with purple hair, the other, a blonde butch cut and a tattooed portrait of a woman on her left upper arm. Both smelled of cheap perfume.

A fat lady with bulging eyes and straggly brown hair was standing behind the counter by the cash register and a brawly black cook, his arms covered in tattoos, was looking out from the kitchen customer window at the frail man on the stool.

"Call the cops, Sue," the young man said to the fat lady. "There's a butchered dead woman in a locked car in the alley."

"Did I hear you right, Travis?" Sue said and leaned over the counter, eyeing him.

"Yeah, call the cops."

"You looked inside the car?" the cook said.

"Through a window. The car was locked, Clint, but I'm telling you, she was butchered."

"Maybe I can open a door," Clint said.

"Leave it alone, it's bad. Let the cops unlock it," Travis said. "Give me a cup of coffee, Sue. They'll be looking for me to give my statement. I'll wait here."

"Maybe she's still alive," Clint said.

"No way," Travis said, shaking his head.

Sue dialed the police and told them what Travis had said.

"They're coming," she said after hanging up. "They said we should stay here. Especially you, Travis."

"Figured that." Travis took a sip of his coffee and frowned. "Probably a whore."

"We ain't going to wait around on no police," the purple-haired prostitute said. "Don't give the cops our names, either."

"Not like we know your real ones anyway," Travis said.

"Keep your mouth shut, creep," purple hair said. The other one nodded in agreement. They both slid off their stools and hurried out.

The sound of sirens filled the street a few minutes later, as a police cruiser turned the corner. Several young women ran past the café, trying to avoid what they thought must be a raid.

The cruiser stopped abruptly in front of the café. Two uniformed cops got out and walked in the front door. One was wearing sergeant stripes on his shirt, with a name tag that read ROLLIE. The other one was younger, taller and twenty pounds lighter than the sergeant. The name on his name tag was WEBSTER.

"Is there a man named Travis in here?" the sergeant asked.

Travis sat his cup down. "That's me."

"The caller said you saw a dead woman in a car," Webster said.

"Yeah, in the alley," Travis said. "The car's locked, looked in the window."

"What's your full name," Rollie said.

"Travis Howard Harlan."

"What were you doing in the alley?" Webster said.

"I work the night shift at the adult movie house across the street. After work I was cutting through the alley to the Ritz Hotel for some shut eye. Must've been about six-thirty this morning."

"Do you know the woman?" Rollie said.

"Couldn't make her out, looks like she's been cut from ass to chest."

"You saw all that, huh?" Webster said. "You took a good look?"

"She was right in front of my eyes. Made me sick."

"This better not be a hoax, Mr. Harlan," Webster said.

"Go see for yourself!" Travis said.

"You two see her?" Rollie asked Sue and Clint.

"No," Sue said. "We've both been right here all night."

"Stay here while we go look," Rollie said. "We'll send someone to talk to you about your customers."

Another police cruiser pulled up behind the first and cut the siren and lights off. Two uniformed cops got out. Sergeant Rollie walked out of the café and met them on the street.

"You two keep a watch on the people in there," he said.

"Will do, Sarge," one of the officers said. "Another call at Suzy's, huh?"

"Always something happening here," Rollie said. "That string bean you see in the window said he found a dead woman in a locked car down that alley over there. We're going to unlock it and have a look. If she's there, I'll call homicide and the coroner. You two make sure no one leaves the scene until I say so. And keep an eye out for anyone suspicious."

The two cops nodded and they all walked in the café.

"Come with us, Travis," Rollie said.

Travis got up and headed for the door.

"Hey!" Sue yelled. "Pay me for the coffee."

Travis started fumbling for money in his pocket, brought out six quarters and laid them on the counter.

"It wasn't fit to drink," Travis said, pushing the quarters toward Sue. "Tastes like you: cold, weak and old."

Sue gave him a dirty look and flipped the bird.

"Stick those quarters up your dirty ass," he said.

"Don't come in here again, dickhead," Sue said to Travis as he walked out.

People were stopping on the street, watching the cops set up in the alley.

Rollie walked up to the car window and looked in.

"Damn. He's right. Tape off the alley, Webster."

"Told you." Travis stepped up to the car and looked in the window again. "That's pitiful."

"Move back from the car," Rollie said. "You ever been arrested?"

"Yeah, a couple of times," Travis said.

"What for?"

"Burglary."

"Then you know the drill," Rollie said. "Turn around and put your hands behind your back."

"You don't think I would be stupid enough to call you if I actually did this, do you?"

"Do what I told you," Rollie said.

Travis turned around. Sergeant Rollie cuffed him and pushed him to the ground.

"Stay put," Rollie said.

"Alright if I go to sleep then?" Travis said.

"Be quiet."

"Exactly what I had in mind."

More curious people were arriving to look at the scene. The sanitation trucks were blocked from entering the alley. The longer the cops stayed, the larger the crowd grew.

Chapter 9

By mid-morning, cops were moving around every-
where in the alley between the adult theater and Suzy's
Café. Annie's body had been put in a coroner's bag and carried away.

As soon as Sunday and Eddy arrived on the scene, reporters began yelling questions at them from the other side
of the yellow police tape.

Eddy turned to Sunday. "The car belongs to a teacher in
Frisco, twenty-five miles from here," he said. "She discovered it was missing last night and called it in. It's being

dusted for prints. Ran a check on her, too, just in case. She's divorced, has two kids. She said she didn't go anywhere in the car last night. Her story checks out so far. No sign of anyone parked in the area that she or the neighbors didn't know, either. Could have dropped someone off and kept going, I guess. There's a bus stop about a block away that runs all night. Someone could have got off the bus and walked back to her house. Had to be someone who knew how to start it without a key. Fingerprints may help. That's where we are so far."

Sunday raised her notepad. "My turn," she said. "Spoke to the man who found our victim. Don't think he knows anything. A crowd of witnesses saw him at the movie theater all night last night. We'll let him go for now. No witnesses on the car in the alley. Victim had a driver's license but no money in her pockets. She's nineteen but, if I had to guess, a lot older street-wise. Witnesses say she's been working here for two or three years. Her name is Annie Chapman. They called her Annie Sweets on the street. Been arrested several times for prostitution and drug use since she was fifteen. Our other victim, Mary Nichols, was college educated, never been in any trouble. As different as you can get. But it looks like it's the same killer. No one here could identify our suspect from the Eagle's Nest murder, either."

"Was afraid of that," Eddy said.

"Something about our suspect's picture looks odd," Sunday said. "Guess it's just the poor quality of surveillance cameras. His features don't seem to match. The black hair sticking out the back of his cap doesn't match the rest of his old face. I'm going to call Mecana. He knows more about these type of M.O's, maybe he can help us prevent another one."

"The new chief may not like that," Eddy said.

"Maybe we don't tell him."

"Probably for the best," Eddy said. "We may not have a job if he finds out."

"You could play dumb, you know."

"Can't let you go it alone."

Sunday smiled. "Ask Barry when he's going to have some prints for us. I'll ask the chief if we can put a few units on patrol around here for the time being. Perp may come back."

"I'll show the night bus drivers in Frisco our suspect's picture," Eddy said and walked towards Eddy and his crew. A wrecker was pulling up to the car to take it to the forensic compound for further investigation.

Sunday stepped away from the crime scene and phoned Mecana.

"H-h-h-hi," Mecana said, breathing hard.

"I didn't interrupt something did I?" Sunday said, ready to hang up.

"No, no. Me and Darcie. Working out. Gym," Mecana said in between breaths.

"Got a minute?" Sunday said. "I wanted to get some advice from you."

"Shoot." He turned on the speakerphone as he and Darcie stepped away from the bikes. "It's Sunday," he said to Darcie in a whisper.

"The monster struck again," Sunday said. "Butchered a prostitute in an alley off Ranch Street last night."

"We saw it on the news this morning, was wondering how you were doing," Darcie said.

"Like to get with you for a talk about it," Sunday said.

"Don't know if we can be of any help," Darcie said, "but we'll be glad to talk with you."

"Have you found the box yet?" Mecana asked.

"No."

"The bag that was in the box is from a time when the same types of murders were happening," Mecana said.

"Let's set up a meeting," Sunday said.

"This would have to be a private meeting between friends," Mecana said. "Don't want to cause any trouble between you and your superiors. Meet us at Brogans for dinner at six tonight."

"I'll be there," Sunday said. "And I'm buying."

Chapter 10

Around noon the next day, a tall muscular man was deleting a police report from his email. The police department sent them automatically to local attorneys. This latest one was about an Annie Chapman. She had been arrested for prostitution and released on bail the day before he murdered her.

He walked in the living room in front of a blazing stone fireplace. Framed pictures of himself and his mother adorned the mantle along with empty candle holders on each end. A large painting of his sad-looking mother with a

Mona Lisa smile and empty brown eyes hung over the fire place.

He removed city sanitation coveralls and blood-covered clothing shoes, cap and a plastic human face. He tossed it all in the fire and watched it burn to ashes, wiping the perspiration from his face with his shirt sleeve. He stirred the ashes with a poker. His cat Truffles was lying on a shag rug near the fireplace and ran away from the heat. He looked up at his mother's painting.

"You didn't even want me to talk to a woman for fear one would replace you. I took care of that. I know what to do with them now."

His phone rang. It was his legal assistant Margi Fletcher.

"Hi Margi," he said. "Glad you're back."

"Can we meet at Brogans for lunch," Margi said. "I have the Winmont report ready."

"I'll be there in about thirty minutes." he said and hung up.

He went to his bedroom and slipped on a fresh shirt, then stopped in front of the fireplace on his way out of the house and again looked at the painting of his mother.

"Margi's just a business acquaintance, mother, nothing personal is going to happen between us."

Half an hour later, he walked into Brogans and saw Margi sitting in a booth.

"Hey Gipson. You hungry?" she said.

"Not really." He sat down opposite her. "When did you get back in town?"

"Came in on a redeye last night." She brushed her long auburn hair back from her big blue eyes. "Saw on the news two women were horribly murdered. It was kind of scary going home alone."

"Don't watch TV much anymore. Too busy."

"You should have a hobby."

"Working on that idea," he said.

A waiter took their drink orders and walked off.

"What did you find out at Winmont?" Gipson asked.

"The same thing is going on in Ashville as here," Margi said. "Employees are being overworked and underpaid, and there have been complaints of sexual harassment. A total mess."

"You talk to Berman about this yet?"

"No. Thought you should know first."

"We'll run it by him Monday and see where we go from here," Gipson said. "It's his law firm, after all."

"Yeah, we're just birds in the nest. This is the best case we had all year. Surely he will turn us loose on it. I can get a dozen witnesses on our side and I have never seen any one better in a courtroom than you."

"Well, you're the best snooping paralegal an attorney ever had."

Margi opened her purse and took out folded sheets of stapled papers.

"Here's a list of names, addresses and phone numbers of women in Ashville who we can call as witnesses. That alone should do it for us."

"Good." Gipson took the paper from Margie and put it in his pants pocket.

"How about I come over this evening and cook a home dinner for your birthday," Margi said.

"How did you know?"

"I know more about you than you do yourself, remember? Happy thirty-sixth. You had to overcome a lot to be where you are today. I'm proud of you."

"That's not helping," Gipson said and smiled at her.

"Oh, I'm so sorry. I wasn't thinking," Margi said. "I'll really have to cook dinner for you now."

"Only if it's not too much trouble."

"It's not. Jerry's been gone six months and mother is going to Vegas with her boyfriend. I'll be by myself."

"I don't ever cook anymore," he said. "All I've got are pots and pans."

"That's okay," she said. "I'll cook and we can spend a pleasant evening together celebrating your birthday. Then we can set up our plan to convince that old grouch Berman to sue for both the wages and the sexual harassment."

"I guess we can do that."

"What's your favorite meal?"

"Whatever you want to fix."

"I'll surprise you," she said. "You know, I haven't been to your house since Berman and I came over last year to celebrate you winning that labor case for the city sanitation employees. That was so cool, them giving you those coveralls and a free parking spot. Made you an 'honorary garbage man.' Every time I think about it I get tickled."

"Me too, but I appreciated it," he said. "That entire case was a lucky win for me. The city ended up giving them a ten percent pay raise."

"Here comes the waiter. You ready to order?"

"Think I'll just have another beer," he said. "Don't want to get too full before our dinner."

"I'll be there around six," she said. "You can pour the wine when dinner's ready."

Chapter 11

Darcie drove her Mustang into Brogans packed parking lot, circled it twice to find what she thought was a safe place for her car, parked and got out. She and Mecana walked to the back of the long line of people waiting to get in. A sign on an easel near the door featured a chalk drawing of a barrel-belly chef wearing a white chef's hat. 'Chef Lorenzo Nadirs, Esquire – One Night Only!' it proclaimed.

Darcie pointed the sign out to Mecana. "I heard he cooked for the Queen of England, too," she said.

"I was wondering why there was a crowd so early."

"We should have met Sunday for lunch, instead."

"If I had known this I wouldn't have offered to pay."

"I think I'll tell Sunday what you said."

Darcie smiled. "You better not!"

They were slowly moving up in the line when Sunday appeared beside them.

"What in the world is happening?" Sunday said.

"Hey you're here," Darcie said, surprised to see her. "Some fancy chef is cooking tonight."

"Explains the crowd," Sunday said. "Eddy's here too, he's trying to find a parking spot."

"You look ravishing in your little black dress," Darcie said.

"You always do in whatever you're wearing. I like you in red," Sunday said. "Want to go somewhere else?"

"Since we're here let's stick it out," Darcie said "May be an experience we'll never have again."

"I know I won't," Mecana said.

Eddy walked up and Mecana shook his hand. They all said hello as they inched forward in line.

"We'll sit up on the veranda for our private talk while we eat some of this royal food," Mecana said. "Does Walt know you're here?"

"No, this is between us," Sunday said.

Once they finally reached the door, the four of them walked up to the veranda, sitting down at a table next to a small tree with drinks in hand, away from the crowd.

"That clerk Dewey said he doesn't have any idea where or when he lost his key," Eddy said. "The lock was hanging on the open gate with no key in it. Forensics is running all kinds of tests in the property room and at Dewey's house. Nothing yet."

"You find anything out about the spike?" Mecana asked.

"It had the markings you described," Sunday said. "Same numbers, too."

"I hoped otherwise but thought it might be," Mecana said. "We never made it known in our report, but that means the killer is using the same bag that once belonged to a suspect in the 1888 Austin Massacres. The same that O. Henry wrote about."

"That's a strange story," Eddy said.

"It is but it's true," Darcie said. "We found it in a secret room at Lisa Durant's mansion but thought it was better to leave out some of the details when we turned it in to the property room."

"So someone who may know the history of that bag could be our murder suspect," Sunday said. "What's worse, we may be employing the person who handed over the box it was in."

"Could be," Mecana said. "Both murders have the same M.O. but we may be dealing with different killers. If just one of them has the bag then it would be the one who murdered Mary Nichols."

"Why? Would he want us to know?" Sunday said.

"That may be as strange as the story I told you," Mecana said. "Dewey may know who, though."

"We've got a century-old puzzle we can't put together," Eddy said.

"Finding the bag will find the killer of the young lady at the Eagle's Nest. Don't know about the prostitute." Mecana said.

"We've already had over ten bogus confessions." Sunday reached in her purse and took out a security camera photo of the man at the Eagle's Nest. "Here's our suspect, but no DNA or ID. You know him?" She handed the picture to Mecana.

He looked at it closely. "No." Mecana passed it to Darcie. She looked at it, then shook her head no and handed it back to Sunday.

"Keep it," Sunday said and Darcie put it in her purse.

"We have to find the bag. That's why I need you," Sunday said. "Thought what you did for me in Mexico would be the last time we worked together, but, here we are again. I think about it often. Something I still have trouble believing is the loss of Angela and Rooster. We wouldn't have made it out without him."

"We think about it too," Darcie said. "I feel so sorry for Rooster. Angela and her family, too. Rooster proved to be a lot more than I think any of us thought he was. He gave his life to give us a chance to escape. We'll always be grateful."

"It's hard to believe Rooster tried to rob me when we met then wound up saving our lives," Mecana said. "We have another dilemma now. The spike came from the bag. Get Walt to sign off on it and we'll take you up on finding the box. We can learn why he's the murderer after we catch him."

"Once I explain this to Walt I'm sure he'll go along with it," Sunday said. "You will be a consultant, officially, and get paid."

Servers came to the table with their food, placing it on the table and pouring more drinks.

"Two conditions," Mecana said once the waiters were gone.

"Name it," Sunday said.

"Add Darcie and DeMax to the consultant list."

"Done. What else?"

"Don't let anyone find out we're looking for the box."

<h1 style="text-align: center">Chapter 12</h1>

Gipson poured wine for Margi and himself. Dinner was ready.

"I hope you like it," Margi said. "It's a combination of several types of Italian food so take your pick or eat some of it all."

"You sure went to a lot of trouble. I do like Italian food and it looks delicious."

"Well dig in. I have a desert for you too," Margi said. "Oh, I almost forgot." She went to the kitchen and retuned with Truffles' bowl and sat it on the floor at the corner of the dining table. "Italian for us, ocean fish for him."

Gipson looked down at Truffles he was eating.

"He likes it," Gipson said. "Now me."

"Bon appétit," she said and smiled.

After dinner, they moved to the couch in front of the fireplace with another glass of wine.

"That was the best dinner I have ever had."

"I could do it again sometime," Margi said.

"I'll give you a break for a while," Gipson said. "I feel guilty for you going to so much trouble. I owe you one. Don't worry, I won't cook it. You pick where you want to go."

"I'll think about it."

Truffles jumped up on the couch and sat down in Gipson's lap.

"He loves you," Margi said.

"Not me, the special food."

Margi laughed. "We can all be bribed if the price is right."

"I've been thinking… I might go out on my own," Gipson said. "Would you be interested in working for me?"

"You should have done that a long time ago," she said. "You do all the work on a case and Berman gets the big bucks because his name is on the sign."

"I was thinking we might take over the Winmont case if you come with me. I'd give you a raise, too."

"They know you're the one who's going to handle it. I don't think they give a damn what name is on the door."

"Okay then," Gipson said. "Send a message to Winmont and I'll turn in my resignation to Berman."

"When will you leave Berman?" Margi said.

"The Rosona drug case is scheduled to go to court next week. I'll resign after that. Should be a cake walk. I spoke to the detectives at homicide, trying to cut a deal with them before I knew the cocaine stolen from their property room was the same the prosecution was going to present as evidence. They don't have any hard evidence now, just heresy. Couldn't be better if I had planned it myself."

Margi slid over on the couch against Gipson, pushing her breasts tight against his chest. Gipson eased back a little from her touch. She reached over and gave Gipson a lingering kiss on the lips.

He didn't know what to do.

Business was one thing, but this was something he wasn't prepared for. She was opening up emotions and memories that haunted him.

It was really all his first girlfriend's fault, back when they were seventeen. His mother forbade him to see girls, but he sneaked off with one in his car and she asked him to make love to her. He tried to have intercourse with her but his mother's voice kept coming to him, repeating what she constantly said all his life. "Stay away from girls, they will ruin your life." He couldn't get an erection. The girl made fun of him and wouldn't stop laughing. He grabbed her by the throat and strangled her. Once she stopped breathing she was his, to do whatever he wanted to now. He could enjoy her without a problem. And he did.

He had grabbed his Boy Scout camping equipment from the trunk of his car and put her in a sleeping bag, then drove to a graveyard. After finding a fresh grave, he dug deep and placed his dead girlfriend on top of the casket and covered everything up with dirt. The shovel he threw in the lake before daylight, then spent the morning vacuuming out his car at a car wash. No one knew she was ever with him, and her body was never found.

Margi broke his train of thought. "I'll clean up the kitchen," she said.

"No, no, you've done enough," Gipson said.

"Being useful makes you feel better."

"Yeah it does."

"I can stay tonight and fix you breakfast in the morning," she said.

Perspiration popped out on his forehead. He fumbled for words. He knew what she was really saying. His heart began to race and he could hear his dead mother's voice. The mere thought of having sex with a live woman was something he had quit thinking about a long time ago. He was trapped. He would have to answer.

"Sure, I've got a spare bedroom."

"That wasn't exactly what I had in mind," Margi said and rubbed his leg.

Gipson looked at her hand. He was wondering if he would have to kill her before, after, or not at all. When he didn't reply she stood up and picked up her purse.

"I'm embarrassed. I made a fool of myself," she said. "I'll leave."

"No, please stay." He couldn't believe what he had just said. He continued, "We're a team. I need you."

"You mean that?"

"Yes. From now on, as long as I'm practicing, I know I can always depend on you."

"Okay, I'll stay."

Gipson forced a smile.

Chapter 13

When Mecana, Darcie and DeMax arrived for their meeting with Walt, Sunday and Eddy were already in his office. Walt looked up and motioned for them to come in. Hand shakes took place and they all sat down.

"So, Sunday tells me you three will help us find the box," Walt said. "And the spike used in the Nichols murder was from the bag, correct?"

"That's right," Mecana said. "They identified it as coming from the Gladstone bag I had left in the box."

"So then, most likely whoever has the bag is our murderer," Walt said.

"I would think so," Mecana said. "I thought the name Mary Nichols sounded familiar to me. And then when Annie Chapman was murdered it hit me: they have the same names as two of Jack the Ripper's victims."

"I'll be damned," Walt said. "Repeating Jack the Ripper…"

"There's some disagreement on who the later victims were, but most believed it was a woman named Mary Kelly," Mecana said. "If we don't find him soon, a woman by that name may be next."

"I'll put out an APB around the entire DFW area." Walt picked up the phone and called in the details to the information officer. He hung up and continued, "In the meantime, I've asked Doctor Seymour to come by and brief us on what the coroner's office has learned. He should be here anytime."

"He's one of the best," Mecana said. "I don't think we would have solved the Durant case without him."

"Once Sunday filled me in on the details, I got the district attorney's office to approve a special consultant contract for the duration of the case for each of you." Walt handed paperwork to Mecana, Darcie and DeMax. "Remember, the only official activity you can pursue is finding police property. You can not make arrests or interrogate suspects without an officer present. Leave that to us."

"You got a deal," Mecana said. The others also nodded in agreement.

Doctor Seymour walked in carrying a manila folder. He looked the part of a doctor, the only thing missing was a white coat and stethoscope. It hadn't been that long since Mecana saw him last. He still looked about the same – a tall, fifty year old with gray hair, wearing a nice blue suit. He always had a slight frown on his face, probably because of the gruesome work he did, Mecana thought. He defied that image by being a friendly, competent coroner.

Everyone stood up as the doctor entered the room. He shook hands with everyone, holding on to Mecana's for an extra moment, then sat down on the brown leather couch, still holding on to the folder.

"Thanks for coming," Walt said. "Mecana's crew is going to hunt for the box I told you about. For the next thirty days we'll be chasing any and all clues you have for us."

"First, let me say this is strictly unofficial. So nothing I say can be put on record," Doctor Seymour said. "You will have an official report from the coroner's office sent to you soon."

"We understand that, Doc, no problem," Mecana said. "I know how thorough you are and what you say is the way it is."

"Mind if we take notes for our own use?" Walt asked.

Doctor Seymour nodded and opened his folder. "That's fine, but keep your notes to yourself," he said. "First, I'd like to start with the spike. From what Sunday told me, it's at least a century old and was hidden in a leather bag inside an evidence box that was placed in the property room by Mecana, correct?"

Mecana nodded.

"The autopsies have been completed and both victims were strangled before being raped and mutilated," Doctor Seymour said. "The knife wounds are from left to right on the throat, with deep cuts in the body, indicating he was right-handed and strong enough to overpower his victims. The bloody size-eleven footprints tell us he's around six feet tall, two hundred pounds. We're running a check on shoe manufacturers now, find out who sells them and trace them to a buyer we think fits the M.O. That'll take some time. We found a lot of different DNA samples on Annie but not too much on Mary. We matched it with three suspects who might fit the description, but all three are in prison. Annie's pimp Tanner Rosana had the most DNA matches and prints. That was expected but he isn't as big a man as what the evidence implies the murderer is, and none of Tanner's DNA or prints were on Mary. Not ruling him out but the facts don't put him in our top suspect category. We're still looking for more DNA. The victims must have known the killer or were completely surprised by the attack. There were no drugs in Mary Nichols' system. Annie Chapman had traces of heroin in her body. The knife wounds were from a broad-base, eight- to ten-inch blade mostly used to butcher animals. Although, this style hasn't been manufactured for at least a hundred years."

"There was that kind of knife in the bag," Mecana said. "The victims also have the same names as Jack the Ripper's first two victims."

"I didn't know that but it doesn't surprise me," Doctor Seymour said. "The same kind of M.O. as the Ripper. Means our killer must know the bag's history."

"What's happening is why we kept it a secret," Darcie said. "But some nut discovered it anyway."

"The profile suggests he probably has a high degree of warped intelligence. He'll be in his late twenties or early thirties, with precise plans to continue murdering women. He has a lot of confidence in himself and left the spike to let us know. What else was in the bag, Mecana?"

"Several things." Mecana began listing them off. "You already know about the spike. There was an eight-inch knife like you just mentioned, an old handkerchief with the initials of one of the Austin victims and a diary from the same woman, documenting her life in Texas. Stamped inside were the owner's initials, the London manufacturer's name, and a date of 1880. Which means it could have been used during the same time period the Ripper committed his murders."

"He didn't leave any DNA or clues except the footprints and the camera shots," Doctor Seymour said. "That may have been on purpose to show us he thinks he's too smart to catch."

"This has echoes of the Durant case," Darcie said.

"It sure does," DeMax said. "If it hadn't been for you, Doc, I would be dead or in prison by now."

"Glad to see you're doing well." Doctor Seymour smiled at DeMax and closed his folder. "That's all I've got for now."

"Thank you very much for coming," Sunday said.

"Yeah thanks," Eddy said. "Now we know more about who we're looking for."

"Good luck," Doctor Seymour said and stood up. "Take care, we have an evil psychopath on the loose."

They all shook hands again and Doctor Seymour walked out of the office with Walt.

"Scary as hell, ain't it," Eddy said.

"Sure is," DeMax said.

"Eddy, can you get me a list of everyone who signed off on anything in the property room over the past six months?" Mecana asked.

"Sure," Eddy said. "We checked them once but maybe you'll see something we missed. I have a report on Mary Nichols and Annie Chapman, too, I can give you. Maybe someone they knew has the box."

"Thanks, email it to us. Anything's possible." Mecana walked over to Darcie and Sunday, who was telling Darcie how much she appreciated her help.

"This guy is totally insane," Sunday said.

"That might be what a shrink would tell you but that doesn't mean he's not normal in other ways," Mecana said. "He could be the last person you'd ever think it was."

"A chilling thought," Sunday said.

"It is," Mecana said. "Follow us to the house, DeMax and we'll make a plan on who does what to find the box."

"Okay," DeMax said. "I have to pick up Mabre from work at the pizza shop first and take her home."

"Bring her with you," Darcie said.

DeMax nodded and they all walked out of the office.

Darcie's phone rang when they walked into the house. It was Amanda.

"Your ex is calling me," Darcie said.

"See what she wants," Mecana said

"Hello." Darcie turned on the speakerphone.

"Tell Mecana Emily can't come now," Amanda said.

"You're on speaker," Darcie said.

"I don't want to talk to him. Just tell him Emily has to enroll in college and find a place to live. Classes start next week. She'll try to come during the holidays."

Mecana snatched the phone out of Darcie's hand. "I can hear you," he said. "You just don't want her to come here. I'll call her."

"It's not my idea. She asked me to call you," Amanda said. "She was afraid you would get upset. Now I see why."

"I'll believe it when I talk to her," Mecana said. "You probably don't want Morgan to visit me either."

"You call her then, smartass," Amada said and hung up.

"She hung up," Mecana said and handed the phone back to Darcie.

"I would have too. You're too upset."

"Disappointed," Mecana said.

"Wait to call her when you calm down," Darcie said. "You don't want to upset her too."

"You're right," Mecana said. "I'll call her tomorrow and tell her I understand."

"That's better," Darcie said. "DeMax will be here soon. Get your mind on a plan to find the box."

"We should have just destroyed it, then we wouldn't have this problem."

"That's hindsight for you. Won't do us any good now."

"Nope." Mecana paused for a moment. "I am a smartass, huh?"

"You said it. I didn't."

Mecana heard DeMax's bike pull in the driveway.

"Back to business."

Chapter 14

Gipson and Margi were sitting at the defender's table in the courtroom when the jury returned with their verdict on Rosona's drug charges. The jury sat down in the jury box and the foreman handed the bailiff a slip of paper, which he handed to the judge.

The judge opened the verdict paper. "Not guilty," he said and slammed down the gavel. "Court dismissed."

Mario Rosona hugged Margi and high-fived Gipson, a big grin on his face.

"You're the best," Rosona said, looking at Gipson.

Gipson shrugged and stuffed papers in his briefcase. "Stay out of trouble, Mario," he said. "I won't be here for you next time."

Assistant DA Bruce Albert walked over to Gipson.

"We're going to file for a retrial, Hayes."

"You lost, forget it," Gipson said. "You had no hard evidence and your witnesses weren't credible. Let's go, Margi."

The two walked out of the courthouse and got in Gipson's Caddy. He didn't start the car, just sat gazing out the windshield like he was somewhere else.

"What's on your mind?" Margi asked.

"Nothing. You need to go home."

"Is everything alright?"

He lied. "Yes. I was thinking about how that would be my last case for Berman."

"You'll get over it once we're on our own," she said.

"Yeah, you're probably right." He started the car and pulled out into the street and went back to his thoughts.

He was wondering what her reaction would be if she found out he was a necrophile. Run? Go to the police? Try to kill him? Maybe she'd think he was joking. He could have a good life with the only live woman he was ever able to have sex with, but the urges to kill were coming again. As a lawyer, he knew if he just fucked the dead and didn't kill them it was legal in many states.

"I have to take my mom to the doctor," Margi said, bringing Gipson back to reality. "She's not breathing well and has been running a temp. Her boyfriend was going to help me but he bugged out."

"I can help."

"Thanks, but I can handle it."

"Do you need any money for the visit?"

"No, we're okay, thank you."

Gipson made a turn on Margi's street and his thoughts of murder returned. Having complete control of a woman like a rag doll was what he wanted right now. Watching her fear and surprise before killing her was the excitement he needed to have sex when she was dead.

"Stop, you're going to pass my house," Margi said.

Gipson slammed on the brakes and stopped a few feet past her driveway.

"Sorry," he said. "I was thinking about evidence research for Winmont."

"You're a workaholic."

"Keeps me out of trouble. Take the week off to stay with your mom. I should have it handled at the office."

"Thanks, Gipson." Margi opened the car door and got out. "Call if you need me," she said. Gipson nodded. She closed the door and walked away.

He drove away but couldn't get the pleasure of murder off his mind. It would be another one in line with his counterparts of the nineteenth century to make it more fun. He would have never thought of it had he not discovered the Gladstone bag. How anyone could be stupid enough to let it out of the property room in such a careless way was unbelievable, he thought. There were some disagreements on the other victims, but he knew he had it close enough the cops would catch on to what he was doing, exactly what he planned.

Instead of turning off to his house, he took the freeway to the little town of Reesville, twenty miles from Dallas, where he grew up. He pulled up in front of the house. His great-grandfather built it long before Gipson was born, at a time when builders still made their houses in an art form, with special carvings and a wrap-around porch to stay cool in the summertime and two fireplaces to stay warm in the winter. Modern A/C units were added once it became available, and the fireplaces hadn't been fired up in years. The windows were boarded up on both floors. The old white paint was peeling off from the second story down. The chain link fence around the house needed repair and the grass was knee-high in the yard. The man he hired to keep it mowed was obviously collecting his fee but not doing his job.

It had been six months since he was here to look for his mother. He thought he got a glimpse of her in her bedroom after she died, but she never reappeared. And she never responded to him going to every room yelling for her.

Growing up he was an only child. Just him and his mother living in the house together. He didn't know who his father was, but there were always men coming and going. His pretty mother claimed she was a princess from some country no one ever heard of, everyone knowing she was making it up. Even Gipson didn't believe her, but he humored her from time to time and would bow when she entered a room. The entire population of Reesville called her a tramp and avoided them both. She was the only friend he had. She died from a stroke when he was twenty, after her doctor and the state had her committed to an insane asylum. He should have sold the house years ago but he always thought she might come back from the dead and still be there, waiting for him.

She left him with a fear of women but he discovered a way to control them. They couldn't hurt him if they were dead, and then he could have his way with them.

He inherited over a million dollars from the estate of his mother's father, a wealthy oilman who passed away from old age when Gipson was a baby. His grandmother ran away with another man and was never heard from again.

He thought he wanted to be an actor in college and enjoyed becoming monsters with special effects makeup like the Hunchback of Notre Dame and the Phantom of the Opera, but he abandoned the make believe world to murder in the real one.

Now things have changed again, he thought. There's a woman he cares for, one who treats him well, maybe even loves him like his mother did, but the urge to kill won't go away. He didn't know how much longer he could hold off.

He turned his car around and headed back to Dallas. He turned off on his street, into his driveway, and went in the house. Truffles ran to him. He reached down and stroked him a couple of times before walking in the kitchen, engrossed with thoughts of who would be his next victim.

He took a sack of dry cat food out of the cabinet and poured some in a bowl. Truffles smelled the dry food, gave Gipson a dirty look and walked away.

"That's all there is," he said and walked back in the den, murder still on his mind.

He noticed the phone book on the coffee table, the same one he used to pick his first two victims. He picked up the book and thumbed through it to the K section. He found four Mary Kelly's, one with a rural address. She would be the easiest if she didn't have a big family. He laid the phone book back on the table.

Truffles jumped on the table, looking at the open phone book, licking his mouth.

"You don't always get what you want, cat, but sometimes it's all you got. I may have to move to another name for my next victim, Truffles. London police had some doubt about Mary Kelly being the third victim, anyway."

Truffles was pawing at the phone book.

Gipson took a beer from the refrigerator, went to his desk, sat down and took a sip. He knew the thoughts of murder would always be his companion. Controlling them was what he hoped to do, or sooner than later he would murder Margi.

Truffles poked his head in the room from the corner of the door, thought better of coming in, and disappeared.

As Gipson went through the evidence Margi accumulated for him, he let the name Mary Kelly slip into his subconscious. He tried to organize a trial plan for Winmont but he always came back to murder when his mother's voice would pop into his head without warning.

Chapter 15

The hunt for the killer was on. Mecana was at the police station with Eddy, DeMax was on Ranch Street, and Darcie was at her home office, searching for similar murders over the last year in the same area.

Mecana and Eddy walked down a flight of stairs to the property room. It had a 'DO NOT ENTER' sign on a locked chain link gate and a fence that ran all the way to the ceiling, blocking off entry to the items stacked on shelves. A camera mounted in the corner recorded the room.

"Sunday said a glob of wet toilet paper was covering the lens," Mecana said. "Did you check the tapes anyway?"

"Yes, a shadow or two, but nothing we could make out," Eddy said. "The camera wasn't where it is now. Before, it was too close to the stairwell, and anyone tall enough could reach it before coming into view. We changed the lock and camera the same day we discovered the box and drugs were missing."

"Does Dewey have a new key?" Mecana said.

"No, just Sunday and Walt now. I've been handling the property room. Walt put Dewey on administrative leave until we find out what happened to his key."

Mecana nodded and waited for him to open the gate.

"Okay, take a look," Eddy said.

Mecana walked in and strolled down the rows of shelves, eyeing them for something out of place or unusual, seeing nothing and walked back out.

"Was this place damaged in any way when the box and cocaine turned up missing?"

"No," Eddy said. "Just the wet toilet paper and a chance they went out the exit door."

Mecana walked over to the exit door and pushed the bar handle down and the door opened. He looked on the outside of the door and there was no handle or door knob. It couldn't be opened from the outside.

"You did run a fingerprint test on the door?"

"We did, but no matches except Dewey and three cops, including me."

"Did you know who had what key?"

"Yeah. Each one had a number. Walt was 34303, Sunday was 34304 and Dewey was 34305."

Mecana wrote the numbers down on a small notepad.

"Sounds suspicious as hell that Dewey would give his key to someone for any reason."

"Yeah, that's our thinking too, but we haven't been able to prove it yet," Eddy said. "He must have been desperate. We find who stole the box and we'll know for sure."

Mecana's phone rang. "Hey Darcie," he said.

"I have the report Eddy sent on Annie and Mary," Darcie said. "Mary and her boyfriend broke up three days before she was murdered, but he was in another state at the time of the murder. Judy didn't hang out with Mary much, she picked Mary up for work and Mary paid her for it. She was well thought of by her employer. No close friends or enemies, only the boyfriend and family. Never been arrested or in any legal trouble. I'm going to run a check on people she or her boyfriend might have come in contact with who could be put in the suspect category. That's going to be a pain in the ass."

"I'll see if Sunday can get the database people to help."

"I'm running a check on murders in the area similar to this one and the Durant case," Darcie said. "Came up with three matches so far from this year. The sickos are always out there. How are you doing?"

"There was no damage. Three people had keys and two of them were Walt and Sunday. Dewey said he lost his key but that's got to be bullshit. But they can't prove it until they find out who has it. Catch-22."

"His key was involved with a crime," Darcie said. "Ask Sunday to get the DA to arrest him as a suspect in the murders. It's probably a long shot but being in jail brings a lot of people to the truth. How's DeMax doing?"

"Oh, you know, he's trying to blend in with the locals, see what happens."

"Bet he's having a ball. I love you," she said.

"Where did that come from?"

"From my heart."

"Made my day," Mecana said. "I'm going to check on DeMax later to see if he's come up with anything. See you tonight. I love you too. You're always in my heart." Mecana put the phone back in his pocket.

"Wasn't trying to eavesdrop, but I heard you say I love you," Eddy said. "I'm working on getting Sunday to say that to me. I spoke to my dad about her. He's encouraging me."

"That's a good start," Mecana said. "What's your dad do?"

"He's a cop in Houston. I was too before I got this job, never dreaming I would find someone like Sunday."

They climbed the stairs headed for Walt's office.

"Sunday here?" Mecana asked as they walked down the hall.

"No, she's out on the trail checking up on the crew," Eddy said. "Walt has patrols staked outside the residences of each Mary Kelly we found."

"This is a game for him and he decided it would be the names of the Ripper's victims," Mecana said. "He made sure we knew he had the bag by leaving the spike. There could even be another Mary Kelly we don't know about. All maniacs like this have one thing in common. They won't stop until we lock them up or they die."

Mecana and Eddy walked into the homicide office but Walt was already gone. He had left a note for them.

"Looks like Walt had a meeting with the police commissioner," Eddy said, reading the note. "The powers-that-be are really starting to put pressure on him to solve the case."

"I know all about that," Mecana said.

Chapter 16

DeMax was sitting at the bar in the Suzy café when Travis walked in. Sue spotted Travis and came out from behind the bar.

"I told you not to come in here again, shit face."

"Oh, come on, Sue." Travis said. "Are you really going to hold a grudge? I was stressed out over finding that dead whore in the alley."

DeMax turned around on his stool and looked at Travis. "You talking about Annie Chapman? Annie Sweets?"

"Maybe. You a cop?"

"Not a cop. Just a PI. I'd like to talk to you. You may have forgotten something when you spoke to the cops that you could tell me."

"Doubt it."

"Was there anyone Annie was fucking that looked like this?" DeMax showed Travis the suspect's picture.

"The cops showed me that. I've never seen him."

"You two get out of here," Sue said.

DeMax laid a hundred dollar bill on the bar. "Will that change your mind?"

"As long as he don't talk to me." Sue pointed at Travis and grabbed the bill.

"That's what I want, too," Travis said, "or you won't get nothin' from me." He walked up to the bar and held out his hand, palm-up.

"You better have an answer to every question I ask," DeMax said. "Or I'll break your scrawny chicken neck."

"Forget the money, then, I'll go."

"Not now, we made a deal. Talk to me and I just might give you the money," DeMax said. "Sit down."

Travis looked at the door like he might run, gave De-Max a frightened look and sat down on the stool.

"Did you know Sweets?" DeMax asked.

"Yeah. I'd seen her around peddling pussy. Was really sorry to hear it was her. Couldn't make her out in the car she was so cut up."

"You see Tanner the night Annie was killed?"

"I ain't talking about him. He'll kill me."

"You hear anything about who might have murdered Annie?"

"I'm not going to talk about that either." Travis gazed off and took a deep breath. "Ask someone else. Leave me alone."

"You tell me what you saw that night or I'm going to stomp your ass."

"I'm going to call the cops."

"Go ahead," DeMax said. "You'll regret it."

Travis grimaced and stared at DeMax.

"I saw him earlier that night from inside the movie house. He was with some new blood he was turning out on the street," Travis said. "The girls looked like teenagers. They didn't know what they were getting in to. I saw him leaving in his ride later with Shelly."

Travis looked up and noticed Sue was listening.

"She's going to tell him I was talking to you. If he kills me, it's your fault."

"Did you see Tanner again that night?" DeMax asked.

"No, man, now I got to go."

"How about you, Sue?" DeMax said.

"I don't know who you're talking about," she said.

"I can get some health inspectors out here. Hate to see what they find. Or you could just tell me what you know about Tanner."

"That's blackmail," she said.

"Sure is. Now, save me some time and tell me."

"I didn't see him at all that night, just this punk," Sue said, motioning towards Travis. "You two get out of my place."

"He still hanging out at the Ritz?" DeMax asked.

"Far as I know," Sue said.

DeMax slapped a hundred into Travis' hand. "Thanks, you can go."

"You're a bad dude," Travis said, looking at DeMax.

"Depends on who you ask."

Chapter 17

Gipson took his phone out of his pocket and dialed Margi.

"Hi," she said.

"Margi, I wanted you to know I've been going through the Winmont files. It looks like a couple of things that happened to a lady named Roberta Sallow is strong enough to make a valid accusation. There's more, too. I'll file it with the court. Might be six months or so before we get a trial date. Why don't you take off some more time to take care of your mother? I'll continue to pay you while we're waiting and get a couple of public defender cases like Rosona's."

"I want to earn my money," Margi said, "but my mother is getting worse. I may not can come back to work for awhile."

"You have earned a fair share of the Winmont case even if you don't do anything else. If we win, we may be looking at several million. You can have half."

"Oh, that's not fair," she said. "You're doing all the work."

"I wouldn't have it if it hadn't been for you coming up with the evidence. That's the way I want it."

"We'll see," she said. "When I can get a break I'll fix you one of those fancy dinners again."

"That would be nice. I'll get the case to court. You need anything, call."

"Thanks I will," she said and hung up.

Truffles jumped up in Gipson's lap.

"Well, looks like we're on our own again," he said to the cat. "I can get back to my hobby."

Gipson grabbed a pen and wrote the address of the rural Mary Kelly in the palm of his hand. He walked back in his bedroom, opened the closet and removed a bright blue cosmetic case and carried it into the bathroom and sat it on the sink cabinet.

He moved the sink cabinet out from the wall, the flex lines uncoiling, and took the Gladstone bag along with a trash bag out of the wall and sat them on the floor. He unlatched the bag and removed the thick knife and his choke rope, looked at them, ran his hand over them slowly like they were pets, and put them back in the bag and closed it. He sat down in front of the bathroom mirror and opened the cosmetic case.

After an hour of applying his mask, he looked up in the mirror. There was an old man staring back at him.

Truffles had been watching all of this. When Gipson looked at him with the old face covering his own, the cat ran away.

"Guess I'll feed you when I get back and look like me again."

He put on clothes over his own and retrieved license plates from the bag he stole. He picked up the Gladstone bag and went to the garage to put the stolen plates on his car.

Forty minutes later, Gipson pulled up outside Mary Kelly's property on the farm road. There was one car parked in the driveway and another sitting across the street. Cops, of course the fucking cops were here, he thought. His anger spilled over and he banged on the steering wheel. He pulled off on a side street, made a u-turn and parked in an empty parking lot. From there, he had a better vantage point of the street.

He waited and watched until she left, cops following close behind her, then followed them to a veterans hospital. Mary Kelly turned into the parking lot, got out of her car and the cops pulled up beside her and watched as she walked toward the entrance of the hospital.

Gipson parked on the street. He walked down the sidewalk and entered the building through another entrance. He made a left turn and walked toward the next door and saw her coming down the hall to an elevator. He turned toward a wall, pretending he was looking at the emergency exit sign on the wall. She stepped in the elevator and punched the fourth floor button. He walked back to where he came in, went back to his car and drove away, rapidly connecting the dots in his head.

She works on the fourth floor, he thought. I'll show them that's where I'll kill her but not tonight.

Most of the way home, he was so upset he kept shaking his head back and forth, like it was on a swivel, and banging on the steering wheel.

"Fucking cops," he said out loud. He almost ran over another car as he sped across lanes to turn off the freeway to his street.

Once he was home, he undressed, removed the old man face and clothes, took a cold shower and put the trash bag and the Gladstone bag back in the wall hideout. He walked into his bedroom naked, laid down on the bed and masturbated.

Chapter 18

Mecana got a call from Sunday.

"Got good news," she said. "Doctor Seymour called. He discovered hair on both victims that he first missed. We've got the new evidence we needed."

"How long will it take to get the results?"

"Not sure but we put a rush on the results."

"That's good news," Mecana said. "DeMax said he may have found evidence that incriminates Tanner the pimp. Wants to meet on Ranch Street. He's been hanging out there for the last three days, watching. I'm on my way there now."

"Let me know. Nothing's happened to any Mary Kellys so far, still keeping watch."

"Stay with them. He's playing a game with us, trying to prove his expertise at murder."

"We'll stay on it."

"By the way," Mecana said, "Darcie mentioned you might try arresting Dewey as an accessory to murder. Scare the hell out of him. Threat of jail time might make him remember who he gave the key to. But check with the DA first."

"Good idea," Sunday said. "Darcie's a brilliant attorney."

Mecana parked on the street and went in the Suzy Café. Two girls jumped up from their table and ran out. Mecana was clean-shave, dressed in expensive jeans and a black polo shirt, the demeanor of a cop in their eyes.

DeMax was sitting at the bar, drinking a beer, the fat lady behind the bar eyeing him. Mecana walked up to De-Max and sat down beside him at the bar.

"Hey Mecana, let's go talk in your truck. Don't seem like I'm welcome here."

He pitched a ten on the bar. They left the café and sat inside Mecana's truck.

"Wanted to see what you thought about what I learned," DeMax said.

"Fire away."

"The guy I called you about is Annie Chapman's pimp," DeMax said. "Tanner something, never got a last name. He beats up his girls when they don't work enough.

Has a natural cruel streak and enjoys it. He wasn't at the hotel yesterday, day or night, and his favorite, Shelly, wasn't on the street last night, either. I knew him from back before you and Darcie saved my ass. Haven't seen him today. Shelly said the guy who picked up Annie flashed five hundred bucks at her and she got in the car. I showed Shelly the photo of the suspect, she said the cops already showed it to her. She didn't get a good look and wasn't sure. Annie didn't have any money on her. He must have taken it back. She's been getting Tanner in trouble with drugs lately. He's been out a lot of money because of her. She's been spending her earnings on drugs and Tanner hasn't been getting his cut. Could be a set up, I know Doc said Tanner didn't fit the profile. But he does fit the place, have a motive, and has spent time with Annie after getting her out of jail the day before she was murdered. Maybe he heard about Mary and wanted to get rid of Annie, too, make people think it was the same guy."

"I see where you're coming from," Mecana said. "Makes sense. It could have been him, which means Mary was murdered by someone else. If so, there's more than one sicko out there."

"That's what I was thinking."

"Sunday mentioned Doc found some DNA on both victims. He's testing it now."

"The fat lady in the café keeps Tanner informed about what his girls are doing," DeMax said. "She knows I'm looking for him."

"He might run," Mecana said. "I'll call Sunday and have her arrest him. Shouldn't be any problem getting a warrant. They can hang on to him for a week, at least, give us time to find out more about this."

"I'm going to go home to Mabre," DeMax said. "This place has too many bad memories for me. I was on a path to nowhere before you and Darcie came along."

"You would have figured it out on your own," Mecana said.

"Maybe." DeMax patted Mecana on the shoulder and walked to his motorcycle. "You need anything, I'm just a phone call away."

Chapter 19

A police cruiser pulled up to the curb at the Ritz Hotel, three working girls on the corner scattered.

Two uniformed officers walked up to the front desk. One was named Brown and the other one Thomas. Brown had a fat face and bulging eyes to go with an overweight body. He kept pulling his pants up. Thomas was slim, a little taller, with blonde hair sticking out from his cap. Both appeared to be veterans with the full swagger of a cop.

"What's your name?" Brown asked the clerk behind the counter.

"Rubin, most days."

"Well it better be the same tomorrow," Thomas said.

"You here for pussy or..." Rubin motioned to the two officers. "Something else?"

"What room is Tanner Rosona in?" Thomas said.

"What you want him for?"

"We've got a warrant for his arrest." Brown sat the warrant on the counter. "Now give us his room number."

"358," Rubin said, "but I don't think he's in now. He's working."

"Give me the damn key." Brown put his hand on the counter, palm up, and wiggled his fat fingers.

Rubin hesitated then placed a keycard in his hand. The officers headed for the elevator.

"That's out of order," Rubin said. "You'll have to walk up."

"You fucking with us, shithead?" Brown punched the up button and the elevator door opened right away.

Rubin threw his hands up, pretending to be startled. "It's a miracle."

"We'll deal with you when we come back," Thomas said.

As soon as the elevator door closed, Rubin phoned room 358. He only said two words, "Run. Cops." He slammed the phone down and shuffled to the front door, disappearing out into the street.

Brown and Thomas got off on the third floor, walked to room 358 and tried the keycard. The lock beeped but the door wouldn't open.

"Bastard gave us the wrong card on purpose," Brown said.

"Think I heard the fire escape ladder drop," Thomas said.

They ran down three flights of stairs, out a side door into an alleyway, as Tanner dropped off a nearby fire escape ladder. He took off running, straight into a tall fence blocking off the alley. He was trapped.

The cops stopped about ten feet from him and drew their weapons.

"Get on the ground, pimp, or I'll blow your shit away," Brown said.

Tanner shifted his feet and looked at the distance to the cops like he was thinking of running.

"Last chance," Brown said, waving his gun at Tanner. "If you don't get on the ground with your hands over your head you're a dead man."

Tanner reached to the back of his belt to try and draw his gun. Both cops opened fire before he could. He fell to the ground, blood pooling around his body.

"I think he's dead," Thomas said.

"Good riddance," Brown said. "Leave him like he is. We didn't have a choice. I'll call it in."

Thirty minutes later, Sunday was taping off the area while Eddy and the forensics crew started doing their job.

Sunday walked up to Brown and Thomas. "You know we'll have to put you on administrative leave until this is investigated."

Both shook their heads yes.

"Will we get paid?" Thomas asked.

"Yes," Sunday said. "File your report. You said he drew down on you, right?"

"Right," Brown said. "We had to shoot."

"Thanks," Sunday said. "Go on home now."

Brown and Thomas walked back to their cruiser and left the scene.

"What do you think about their story?" Eddy asked Sunday.

"I believe what they said."

"Tanner's got a brother named Mario who's even worse then he is," Eddy said. "Don't have a warrant on him, though, he was acquitted on his drug charges."

"I called him," Sunday said. "He said he didn't have anything to do with his brother, that he wasn't going to bury him and to not ever bother him again. Didn't surprise me. Their father is doing life in prison for murdering their mother. They grew up on the street dog-eat-dog. Wonder why Tanner thought he had to shoot his way out?"

"Hard to figure," Eddy said. "Maybe he thought we'd link him to Annie's murder. Even if it wasn't him, we're likely to find his DNA on her."

"We need hard evidence, like the knife or whatever he strangled her with. If we find his DNA on Mary, too, we'll know it's him."

"That would do it."

"Find out what forensics has on this."

"Sure. You never know until you know." Eddy grinned and walked away.

Sunday stood there looking at Tanner's lifeless body, deep in thought.

"We're still chasing a ghost."

Chapter 20

The next day, the buzzer at the morgue rang and a little man with glasses and a white coat unlocked the door and cracked it open.

A tall man with thick, black wavy hair and dark brown eyes was standing there, handcuffed to a uniformed police officer even bigger than he was.

"The cops made me come down here to ID my brother, Tanner."

The little man looked at the cop.

"Let us in, Billy," the cop said. Billy opened the door and they walked in

"Follow me," Billy said and they walked down a row of metal doors. He stopped at one labeled #39, grabbed the handle and pulled a body out on a tray.

He pulled the sheet off the face of the dead body. "Yeah, that's Tanner. Can I go now?"

"Sign the sheet and you can go," the cop said.

He scribbled the name Mario Rosona.

"Get the coroner to sign his John Hancock on that and send a copy to homicide,

Billy."

They walked back to the door. Billy unlocked it and let the two men out. The cop stopped in the open door.

"Why do you keep the door locked?" the cop asked.

"People steal bodies," Billy said. "Especially women."

"I'm sorry I asked."

Mario Rosona stopped at the Ritz hotel. Rubin was back behind the counter.

"I'm Tanner's brother. I'm here to get whatever he has left. What room was he in?"

"Room 358," Rubin said. "Someone already stripped it, though. Nothing left."

"You know who did it?"

"Not sure," Rubin said. "Someone did it before the cops came back when I wasn't here."

"Bullshit. You know word travels fast." Mario reached behind his back, pulled out his snub-nose and placed the barrel against Rubin's head. "Now, tell me who took his stuff or say hello to Tanner."

"The bitches from his stable must have. Wasn't me."

"I'll have a look anyway, give me the key." Mario lowered the gun and Rubin handed him the key.

Mario walked to the elevator and stepped off on the third floor. Room 358 was the first door on his left. He opened the door and walked in. All of the drawers from a chest and tables had been dumped on the floor. The mattress pushed off the bed and cut open. Nothing left of any value.

"Shit," Mario said as he kicked a drawer over and noticed a key taped to the bottom. He took the key off and looked at it. It had the words SURELOCK on one side and the numbers 34305 on the other side.

The first thing he thought of was a bank box with money in it. He stuck the key in his pocket and went back down to the front desk. Rubin put his hands up over his head.

"I told you I didn't have nothing to do with it."

"You ever hear Tanner say anything about a bank?"

"I don't know what you're talking about," Rubin said. "Never heard him mention anything about a bank, he always used cash from his whores."

"If I find out you're lying I'll be back."

They heard a woman's high heels and looked around. Shelly was walking in with an old man with a smile on his face. Rubin reached under the counter and handed her a key when she got to the counter.

"You getting an early start to the day, Shelly?" Rubin said. "Thought you would go to Tanner's funeral."

"He's not having one," Shelly said. "The state is going to put him in a pauper's grave soon. He didn't leave me nothing."

"You Tanner's girl?" Mario asked.

"Don't nobody own me," Shelly said. She put an arm around the old man and walked him to the elevator.

"After you turn your trick I want to talk to you," Mario said.

"I got nothing to say to you motherfucker," Shelly said.

Mario ran to her and slapped her down. The old man swung at him, but Mario gave him an uppercut and he fell to the floor out cold.

"You son of a bitch," Shelly said, kicking at Mario. He backhanded her and she hit the floor again.

"Leave her alone, Mario," Rubin said.

"Shut up or I'll kick your ass, too."

"I'm going to kill you," Shelly said, rubbing her face.

"You don't tell your target before you do, stupid," Mario said. "I might decide to do away with you first. Now, do you know if Tanner had a bank account or savings box at any bank?"

"No, I don't." Shelly staggered to her feet. "Look what you've done," she said, pointing at the old man on the floor.

"Why don't you just take his money and disappear."

"Yeah, just get out of here, Shelly," Rubin said.

Shelly stared at Mario then bent down and removed the old man's wallet from his pocket.

"I'll get even with you," she said, still looking at Mario. She turned around and ran out of the back of the hotel.

Mario walked out the front door, got in his car and started to pull away from the cub when a police cruiser blocked him in. Two young cops jumped out with pistols drawn, yelling at him.

"Get out of the car and put your hands over your head," one of the officers said. "Try anything and you'll end up like your brother."

Mario slipped his gun out of his belt and laid it on the seat so he wouldn't be armed. If they shot him it would be murder as last revenge.

He leaned up against the car, put his hands on top of it and spread his legs. He was very familiar with the routine.

"You're under arrest," the cop said. "We've got evidence this time."

They handcuffed him and sat him in the back seat.

"I want my phone call," Mario said.

They didn't answer so Mario repeated himself.

"I have a right to call my lawyer."

The cops still didn't answer him, just talked about which football games they would watch over the weekend.

Mario ran his handcuffs across the metal grill on the back of the front seat, making a horrible noise. The cop on the passenger side glanced back at him.

"Cut that shit out," he said and they went back to talking about sports.

Chapter 21

Mecana and Sunday sat looking through the one-way mirror into the interrogation room. Eddy was in there speaking to Mario Rosona. Sunday thought they had a lead on Dewey's missing evidence room key.

"This guy is Tanner's brother," Sunday said. "We had to force him to identify Tanner at the morgue yesterday. He swears he found the key in Tanner's hotel room on the bottom of a drawer after someone had ransacked the room. The key had Dewey's numbers on it."

"I know of him," Mecana said. "That's where he belongs, whether he has the key or not."

"Him and his brother were sworn enemies," Sunday said. "We have a witness that will testify he was with Mario when he made a million dollar deal to buy cocaine from a cartel. It will be a retrial, his lawyer got him off the charge the first time when the drugs disappeared with the box we're looking for. We've got a witness this time, though. We know he's not the killer. He was in jail when both Mary and Annie were murdered."

"DeMax could be right," Mecana said. "Maybe Tanner got the key from Dewey, stole the box and someone else got the bag. The murders are so similar. If Tanner is a copy cat then we have two killers."

"We have a close watch on the Mary Kellys," Sunday said. "We should be getting the DNA report soon. Hopefully it's a match to someone in the database."

Sunday flipped on the microphone switch in the interrogation room. Eddy was speaking. "We've got a witness that was with you, saying you made a deal with the cartel," Eddy said. "Did you also steal drugs and evidence from our property room?"

"I told you, I found the key at Tanner's. That's all I know about it. I thought it was a bank key."

"Where did you get that idea?"

"I'm not saying another word. I want my lawyer," Mario said.

"Who's that?"

"Gipson Hayes."

Sunday turned off the mic.

"Hayes was the public defender for Rosona on that drug deal." Sunday said.

"Have you run a check on the lawyer?" Mecana said.

"Yes, he's a well-respected attorney with a great re-cord." Sunday opened a folder and read from it. "Only one conviction out of 75 clients he represented in the last five years. He was at the top of his law class, born and raised in Reesville. No arrest or connections to any criminals. No DNA in the database. He represented Rosona as a public defender pick. Not his choice but his obligation as an attor-ney."

"Just happened to be Rosona," Mecana said

"I have some men at Rosona's apartment now looking for evidence. We might need to convict him if something happens to our witness. We're going to try and get a confes-sion before we jail him."

"Well, from what you said, you might need it if Hayes represents him," Mecana said. "I'll ask Darcie how that works."

"Mario had a .38 in his car. We'll run a ballistic check on it."

"I'm going to have a talk with Dewey," Mecana said. "Darcie had the department run a check on his days off and there were two. One matched the time the box and drugs were discovered missing. Trouble is, nothing was officially checked out on those days, so we don't have a suspect other than Dewey. Maybe he went in and no one saw him, or maybe he gave someone the key for money."

"We could use a break." Sunday flipped the interroga-tion room speaker back on and Mecana walked out to his truck. He checked Dewey's address in his notepad and drove that way.

The address was on a street with a row of old brick houses that had been kept up with over the years. Probably owned by the tenants. Dewey's house had a white picket fence around the front yard. Two cars were parked in the driveway.

Mecana walked up to the front door and rang the door bell. No one answered. He rang it again. Still no answer. He stepped over to a window and looked in. No one in the room. He tried the door bell again. No one came to the door. He walked around to the back of the house and saw the back door was slightly open. He drew his Glock and entered the house.

Inside was a foul smell he recognized. He walked down the hall to a bedroom, the smell coming through the cracked door was even stronger. He pushed the door open with the barrel of his gun. A woman was lying in the bed, a pool of blood around her and Dewey, who was draped over her lower body wearing nothing but pajamas and a hole to the head.

Mecana listened for any sounds and continued searching the house. When he didn't hear or see anyone he put his gun away. He went back to the bodies. No question they were dead. They were turning purple. Rigor mortis had already set in.

He reported what he found to the police and waited on the front porch. He wanted to check Dewey for the property key but knew it wouldn't be a good idea to leave any fingerprints.

By the time the first ambulance showed up, so did Robert Chandler and Kimber Blount. The two men walked up to Mecana. He noticed Chandler and Blount weren't as thin as they used to be. Work and marriage must have been keeping them from the gym, he thought.

"We heard your call on the scanner," Chandler said to Mecana. "You and murder are old friends."

"You may be my next victim, asshole, if you don't back off," Mecana said.

"You're talking to police officer. Mind your tongue before I arrest you."

Blount stepped between them. "What are you doing here anyway, Mecana? You're not a cop anymore."

"Her about the missing evidence. I found two dead in the bedroom. That's all I've got to say to you."

Chandler and Blount looked at each other. Blount motioned toward the door. They reached in their pockets and put on a sanitation mask and walked in the house through the open door.

Mecana stepped off the porch and walked out into the front yard and called Sunday.

"Hey," Sunday said. "We heard it on the monitor. Both dead?"

"Yes. They're turning purple. Now we know why Tanner was running. Think evidence will show he kill them. Tanner was the one with the key. No doubt he's our box thief. But who in the hell has the bag?"

"He was afraid Dewy was going to spill the beans."

"Seems to add up that way," Mecana said. "Chandler and Blount showed up. You going to leave them on this?"

"That's Walt's call. He probably will since they were first on the scene. Doesn't change anything with us, though. Barry and his crew will do the important work anyway and give us a report."

"Those two are dangerous."

"They think you are, too."

"That's not surprising," Mecana said.

"By the way, Mario keeps asking to call his lawyer."

"You mean Hayes?"

"Yeah," Sunday said. "We called but he said he doesn't want to represent him. Apparently last time wasn't his idea either, but a judge still might assign him as a public defender since he's represented him before on the same charge."

"I'll stop by."

Mecana hung up the phone and saw Barry and his forensic crew had arrived. Several headed for the bedroom. Barry stopped to talk to Mecana.

"Sunday said you called this in and to get in touch with her before giving Chandler and Blount a report."

"We don't want it messed up," Mecana said.

"Don't have anything to say about that. Except I got a call from my superior to send it to her first and that's what I'll do." Barry grinned and started walking away.

"Thanks, Barry. I saw a .45 casing lying on the floor, should match the murder weapon."

Barry nodded and kept walking.

Chandler hurried out of the house. "We're going to need a statement on this, Mecana," he said.

"I'm on my way to see Sunday now, we're going to talk all this over. I'll fill in the blanks for her."

"We need it now," Chandler said.

"Get out of my way. I'll give it to Sunday," Mecana said. "I still remember those trumped-up murder charges you tried to pin on me. You knew it was a clean kill. Those assassins were trying to murder Candy Kane. Thank goodness Robert straightened you out."

Chandler let his anger show as Mecana walked away.

"You're gonna fuck up one of these days, Mecana. And when you do, I'll be there to hang your ass."

Chapter 22

Gipson was up late working on evidence for the Winmont case, trying to keep his mind off Mary Kelly. His phone rang, it was Margi.

"Glad you called," Gipson said. "I've been working on the case and we have a very good chance to win."

"That's great news," Margi said. "Really great. But...I can't work for you anymore. My mother has lung cancer and I'm going with her to Arizona for treatment. I'm sorry."

"Can't you make other arrangements? I need you. In more ways than one. I was counting on you."

"I have to go. We're on our way to the airport now. I'm so sorry."

Gipson stood up and slammed his fist on the desk.

"What was that noise?" Margi asked.

"You lied! It's like my mother said, a man can't trust a woman. Go on, bitch. If you come back you'll be sorry."

"I knew your mother was insane, Gipson, but it sounds like you are, too," Margi said. "Don't ever call me again."

Gipson grabbed his computer monitor and threw it against the wall, breaking the glass. Truffles jumped up and ran out of the room.

"She's like all the rest!" He flopped back down on his chair and put his hands to his face, crying. After a few minutes of sobbing he wiped his eyes and stood up, anger boiling over.

He walked to the bathroom and removed the Gladstone bag from the wall. He sat down on the stool and opened his makeup kit. He began to add wrinkles and age spots to his face, painted his eyebrows gray, and enlarged his nose.

He looked in the mirror and saw a septuagenarian looking back at him.

"None of you deserve to live," he said to the mirror.

With a change of clothes, a pair of gloves and a knife, Gipson walked to his car and headed for Berman's law firm.

Gipson pulled into a parking space that still had his name on it. Before he got out, he taped a trash bag under his jacket and adjusted it to look like a fat stomach. He walked out to the street and sat down at the bus stop. Once the next one came along, he rode for thirty minutes with no destination in mind, just looking for a woman of opportunity.

Several stops later, two young women dressed in waitress outfits sat in the seat behind him. They both were pretty, in their twenties. The blonde had the window seat and the brunette the aisle. He overheard them talking.

The brunette said, "I'm glad that shift is over."

"Your boyfriend home?" the blonde asked.

"No, he had to go to Chicago for a seminar."

"You want me to spend the night with you?"

"I'll be alright. I got a gun and know how to use it," the brunette said. "My stop's coming up, see you tomorrow."

"Yeah get some rest," the blonde said.

The brunette got off at the next stop and Gipson followed her off, but turned in the opposite direction. He walked down to the end of the block and stopped, turning back to watch her walk down the dark street. The bus had already headed for its next destination. No one else was on the street.

He turned around and followed her at a distance. She turned on the next street toward an apartment building and he began closing the distance between them. He watched her walk up to a door on the ground floor apartment with drapes drawn across a window. She unlocked the door, reached in and flipped on the light switch. No one else in view.

Gipson bolted around the corner and pushed her through the doorway. She dropped her purse on the floor. It flew open and a snub-nosed .38 fell out. He kicked the gun away and cut off the lights. The brunette tried to run through the open door but he grabbed her around the neck before she could get away, putting a choke hold on her. She screamed but his arms were cutting off her wind pipe and it came out as a whisper. He kicked the door shut and hung on with a death grip as she struggled to get free. He squeezed the life out of her and she collapsed in his arms. He dropped her on the floor, took the trash bag from under his clothes and pitched it away from her. He propped her up in a corner and stretched her legs out. He drew the knife from his belt, pressed it deep into her throat, sawing on it until her head fell off, blood covering her body, his gloved hands and clothing and shoes. He placed her hands in her lap palms-up and sat her head in her hands, pressing her closed eyes open with his thumb and index finger.

"That's better," he said, looking at her open, glazed brown eyes. He wiped his knife off on her uniform under her 'Tillie' name tag and stuck the knife back in his belt. He stepped away from her, removed his bloody clothes and very carefully folded them and placed them in the trash bag after removing the clean clothes. He put on skin-colored gloves and a gray toupee from his clean jacket pocket and adjusted them both, then made another fat belly by pushing the trash bag around under his clothes.

"Time to go. Can't wait for the cops to see you," he said, staring at her posed headless body. "Wish it was you, Margi."

Chapter 23

In the wee hours after the murder, Mecana rose up in bed, wide awake.

"I'll be damned," he said, staring into his dark bedroom.

Darcie turned on the bedside lamp.

"You woke me up," she said. "What are you mumbling about?"

"DeMax mentioned someone named Shelly. Tanner's main squeeze, I think. If he had the key, then she would know how he got it and who has the bag now."

"That suddenly came to you in your sleep?"

Mecana stood up in his underwear, went to his closet and started getting dressed.

"What are you doing?" Darcie asked.

"I'm going to pick up DeMax and go look for Shelly. These are her working hours, after all."

"I'll go with you."

"No, the whores might attack you if they think you're the new competition."

"I don't know if that's a compliment or an insult."

"A compliment, naturally, because you're so gorgeous." Mecana smiled at her as he dialed.

DeMax answered the phone. "Something bad happen?" he asked.

"We need to find Tanner's girl Shelly."

"At two in the morning?"

"Tanner stole the box but someone else has the bag," Mecana said. "She would know who. I'll pick you up in thirty."

"Alright, but you're gonna have to explain to Mabre. She wasn't too happy about me spending all that time with the whores, not sure I'll survive a second trip out there."

"I may have the same problem," Mecana said and hung up.

He turned to Darcie. "Keep your Beretta in the bed with you, honey, until I get back." He gave Darcie a quick kiss and hurried out the door.

An hour later, Mecana and DeMax were walking in Suzy's Café. There was only one other person besides Sue in the restaurant – a young woman wearing skimpy clothes, slouched in a corner booth, head down and eyes closed.

"That girl okay?" Mecana asked.

"She's sleeping," Sue said. "What are you two doing back?"

"We're looking for Shelly, seen her?"

"Kiss my ass."

"Ain't that desperate," DeMax said.

"You seen Shelly?" Mecana asked again.

"Which one? Know several Shellys."

"You know who we're talking about," DeMax said. "Tanner's girl."

"Heard she quit the street," Sue said. "Buy something or leave."

"Where is she now?"

"What you want to know for, you're not a cop."

"We can find one if you don't tell us."

"I don't know, try Rubin at the hotel."

"What you think, DeMax?" Mecana said.

"She's been working the beds there for the last two years," DeMax said.

"Lets go then," Mecana said.

"Yeah, get the hell out of my place," Sue said.

"You got a real attitude problem, lady," Mecana said, shaking his head as they left.

Outside, the skinny sax player was still sitting on the street in front of the movie house, playing his saxophone.

"Let's take a walk over there and talk to Blaster," De-Max said. "Shelly was always giving him money."

"The sax player?"

DeMax nodded and they walked across the street.

Blaster took the reed from his lips when he saw DeMax and laid the sax in his lap.

"Well, well, well. You finally come home, DeMax," Blaster said. "Saw you the other day but you didn't come to see me. Heard you was a detective now, big shot. Too busy to say hi?"

"Yeah, sorry," DeMax said. "Been working."

Blaster coughed and wiped the perspiration from his face with the back of his skinny hand, then brushed his long hair back from his forehead. His legs and feet were twisted out of shape. A pair of crutches behind him.

"You seen Shelly today?" DeMax asked.

"Nope. She done quit us since the cops killed her man. Gonna try and be an upright citizen or something. She was kind of whored out anyway. If she had as many dicks sticking out of her as she had stuck in her she'd look like a porcupine." He gave a good laugh at his own joke then looked at Mecana. "Do I know you?"

"Not exactly, but you may have seen me," Mecana said. "Used to be a cop. Retired now, though."

"That's it," Blaster said. "Thought there was something about you I didn't like."

"He's a good friend. Saved my ass once or twice," De-Max said. "You know where Shelly went?"

"Think she said her mother's. Didn't get a name or town," Blaster said. "But I wouldn't tell you even if I did know. You're not one of us anymore, DeMax."

Mecana reached in his pocket and dropped a hundred dollar bill in Blaster's cap.

Blaster picked up his sax and blew the first five notes of the national anthem and sat the sax back in his lap. "There's your money's worth," he said and smiled.

Mecana smiled back. "Let's check the hotel."

"See you, Blaster," DeMax said.

Blaster picked up his saxophone again, blew a long, rough-sounding note and sat it back in his lap.

At the hotel, a working girl and a middle-aged, sloppy-looking John were coming out of the elevator. They both stopped and stared at Mecana and DeMax until they walked on by, then gave a sigh of relief and left the hotel in a hurry.

No one was at the front desk. A sign propped up on the counter read, "If you already have a room go on up. If you don't go away. Rubin."

Mecana walked around behind the counter and banged on the door behind it, but no answer.

DeMax stepped up to the door and took a turn pounding on it.

"Get your ass out here, Rubin, or I'm gonna huff and puff and kick your door down!"

Mecana grinned. "That should do it," he said.

The door opened and Rubin was standing there in his heart-covered boxer shorts.

"What the hell do you two want?"

"Where's Shelly Taylor?" DeMax asked.

"She left this afternoon, said she was done here and won't be back." Rubin was pushing the door, trying to close it.

DeMax stuck out his foot to block the door.

"Where did she go, Rubin?"

"I don't know. Let me get some sleep."

"She's been here at least two years," DeMax said. "You know where she goes when she's not working."

"To her mother's I think."

"What's her mother's name?" Mecana asked.

"I think she said Ruby. Ruby Taylor. Same last name as Shelly's. She's got a young daughter her mother keeps for her. I don't know where she stays, though. That's the truth."

"You're sure her mother's name is Ruby Taylor?" Mecana asked.

"Yeah that's it," Rubin said. "Now get your damn foot out of my door, DeMax."

DeMax looked at Mecana.

"If that's her name we can find her," Mecana said.

DeMax took his foot out of the door and Rubin closed it.

Mecana and DeMax left the hotel and Mecana called Darcie.

"Are you okay," Darcie asked.

"Yeah, what about you?

"Fine. What's happening out there?"

"I need you to look up a Ruby Taylor. She's Shelly's mother. Think that's where Shelly went to. Her mother's probably in the city somewhere. She watches Shelly's kid so it's probably not too far away. Unfortunately, Taylor is a very common name."

"Okay, I'll see what I can find and get back to you," Darcie said. "Couldn't sleep anyway."

Chapter 24

Darcie came up with three possibilities. Mecana and DeMax left near dawn to check the first one at a trailer park. The name Taylor was on the mailbox. No lights were on in the small trailer. An old silver Toyota Corolla was parked in the driveway and a newer-model red Ford Taurus sat on the street in front of the trailer.

Mecana stopped across the street, turned off his headlights and left the truck running.

"What now?" DeMax asked.

"Thinking it over," Mecana said. "They could have us arrested if we break-and-enter and I don't want to call the cops until we find Shelly. This is a likely place. They're not going anywhere 'til daylight. Let's wait until dawn."

Once the sun was up, they decided to try the trailer again. A light was now on.

They walked up to the door and Mecana motioned for DeMax to step back and he knocked on the door. No one came so he knocked again. A woman pushed a curtain back on the door window and looked out with big blurry eyes at Mecana and quickly closed the curtain.

"We're looking for Shelly Taylor," Mecana said through the door. "Is she here?"

"What you want," a woman's voice said through the door.

Mecana smiled. They found her on the first try.

"Go away, asshole," a different woman's voice said.

DeMax stepped up to the door. "You need to talk to us before we have to call the cops. You don't really have a choice. It's us or the cops."

"The guy at the door a cop?"

"No, he's a private eye. We just need to ask some questions about Tanner," DeMax said. "If you come clean you may not have to go to jail."

"Guarantee me I won't be arrested and I'll talk to you."

"We can't do that," Mecana said. "But if you don't talk to us we'll have to call the cops."

"He's right, Shelly," DeMax said. "You're better off with us."

The door came open and Shelly was standing there in a red housecoat, her hair tied in a ponytail. She pulled the coat tighter around her and stepped back from the door. Mecana and DeMax walked.

"Okay," she said. "What do you want to know?"

The older woman picked up a pack of cigarettes off a coffee table and took her granddaughter to another room. Shelly sat down on a floral-patterned chair and Mecana and DeMax sat down on a small black leather couch pushed up against the wall.

"I'll get right to the point," Mecana said. "Tanner stole an evidence box and drugs from the police station property room. We know he had the key to the property room and there's a very good possibility he murdered the evidence clerk Dewey and his wife. You could be charged as an accomplice to murder. Tell me about it."

Shelly dropped her head and tears fell to the floor. She raised her head and wiped the tears from her eyes.

"If I tell you, will you help me keep my daughter?

"Give me the complete story as you know it," Mecana said. "We'll do what we can."

"That true?"

"His wife's a lawyer," DeMax said. "She saved me from all kinds of hell."

"Dewey made a deal with Tanner," Shelly said. "Tanner gave him ten grand for the key so he could steal the drugs on Dewey's day off. I got arrested that day on purpose, and Tanner came to bail me out. He was doing that for all his girls so it didn't look suspicious for him to be there.

"He went to the restroom and came out with a wad of wet toilet paper in his hand. No one was in the hall to see us. He stuck the toilet paper on the camera before we were in view, opened the gate to the property room and grabbed the box. He took the bag out and handed it to me and filled the box with cocaine. We never opened the bag.

"He told me to put the bag in the dumpster when we left the building. I couldn't raise the heavy dumpster door with one hand so I just sat the bag down in front of the dumpster. Then we hauled ass out of there."

"What time was that?" Mecana asked.

"About three that afternoon, or so."

"Do you know who picked up the bag?"

"No. It was sitting there when we left. That's the last time I saw it."

"What did he do with the drugs?"

"I don't know," Shelly said. "Sold or traded them, probably."

"Did Tanner kill Dewey and his wife?"

"He said Dewey wanted more money. I didn't know he was going to kill them, I swear. I wasn't even with him."

"You did the right thing, Shelly," DeMax said.

"I'll have to call the cops to arrest you for your part in this but I'll call my wife to see if she can get bail for you," Mecana said. "Can your mother take care of your baby until we can get you out?"

"I'll get dressed," Shelly said.

"DeMax, stay with her. I'll go outside and call Sunday and Darcie."

"Okay," DeMax said.

Mecana got up and headed for the door and they heard sirens screaming in the distance as he walked out.

Mecana hadn't been gone five minutes and came hurrying back inside.

"There's been another murder," Mecana said. "When I called Sunday she said they got a call to 4319 Dickens Street. Sunday and Eddy are on the way. The sirens we heard must've been heading there. I'm going to go and see what we have. Hold on to Shelly. I'll call you a ride and you take her to the police station for booking. Then wait for me and Darcie to get there."

"You got it," DeMax said.

Mecana hurried to his truck and drove away.

A crowd had gathered by the time Mecana got to the murder scene. It was taped off. Six police cruisers, an ambulance, the coroner's wagon, forensics officers, Sunday and Eddy's cars were all parked in front. Mecana walked up to the tape. A young officer was patrolling to keep people out.

"My name's Mecana," he said. "I'm working with Sunday, can I go in?"

"Not unless they tell me you can," he said.

"Would you tell them I'm here?"

"Can't leave the tape right now. Reporters trying to get past to take pictures."

Sunday appeared and waved him inside to the room.

Inside, a sheet was covering the victim, blood on the edges of the sheet. Sunday raised the corner up. Mecana took a quick look and she dropped it back down.

Mecana grimaced and shook his head.

"This is the worst one yet, but no doubt it's the same killer," Sunday said. "But not a Mary Kelly. Her name is Tillie Moncreate. Her boyfriend found her this morning when he got back from Chicago. By the estimated time of death, he was still in Chicago when she was murdered.

"As you can see there's bloody shoe prints, same size but a different shoe sole. That makes three different types. We're searching for where the shoes were purchased. Eventually we'll find him, but he may kill a dozen more before we do.

"We've got the DNA back from the hair on both victims but we can't find a match. He strangled her, cut off her head and posed her so when anyone opened the front door she would be the first thing they would see, holding her head in her lap. Most disgusting thing I have ever seen.

"If Shelly Taylor confessed to being with Tanner when he stole the box and bag, at least that's some progress."

"She did," Mecana said.

Eddy walked up. "Hey Mecana. Never seen one this bad. Having trouble keeping breakfast down."

"Sunday was telling me about it. He couldn't wait for a ripper victim. He had to kill now."

"It's so frustrating," Sunday said.

"Sometimes staying busy helps," Mecana said. "A lot of cases have taken years to solve."

"I know, it's just so incomprehensible that a human mind could be this sick," Sunday said.

"They have always been out there and always will be," Mecana said. "I'm going to run by the station and check with Darcie to see what the deal is with Shelly getting bail. I promised I would."

"Okay," Sunday said. "I'll call you when we get done here. No doubt it's the same killer. He just quit playing the Jack the Ripper game."

Chapter 25

Darcie and DeMax were waiting in a courtroom for a judge to hear Shelly's request for bail when Mecana walked in. A door came open and a bailiff brought Shelly in, wearing an orange jumpsuit with her hands cuffed in front of her. The bailiff un-cuffed her and sat her down in front of a court bench.

Darcie saw Mecana and waved for him to join them.

"Looks like I got here just in time," Mecana said.

"She's been charged with theft, prostitution, perjury and as an accomplice to a homicide. She said she wasn't with him when he killed Dewey and his wife so I contested the accomplice charge," Darcie said. "Not going to be easy or quick but I know this judge, he has always been fair."

The door opened behind the judge's desk and a short gray-haired man in a judge's robe walked in. He had his glasses pushed down on his large nose, glancing at a paper he had in his hand and stepped up on the desk platform.

The bailiff said, "All rise." Everyone stood up waiting for the judge to sit down. When he did, everyone else followed.

The judge cleared his throat and directed his attention to Darcie.

"Well counselor, it's been a while since I've seen you in my courtroom," he said.

"Haven't been practicing, your honor, until this came to my attention."

"What I have here is a request for bail for Shelly Taylor."

"Yes, your honor."

The judge looked at Shelly. "Please state your legal name, young lady."

"Shelly Ann Taylor."

"Counselor, I see she has been arrested several times for prostitution and other misdemeanors. The charges this time are far more serious. Felonies, even. You may present your request for bail."

"Yes, your honor. She's a single parent and wants to find a legal and moral way to put her life together and raise her daughter. I believe she's sincere and will change her life for the better. Shelly denies having had anything to do with the murder and has an alibi. She was working at the time."

"Working?" the judge asked

"At her profession."

"Oh, that profession."

"Yes, she has no objection to reporting weekly for accountability and proof she's no longer pursuing that profession."

The judge picked up the paper from his desk and looked at it and laid it back down.

"Because some of the charges are felonies, bail will be set at one-hundred thousand dollars. Miss Taylor, do you understand the conditions of bail?"

Shelly stood up without being prompted. "Yes, your honor."

"If you are charged with any other crimes, or fail to appear for your trial, you will be arrested and confined. Do you understand?"

"Yes your honor," Shelly said.

"Very well. Good to see you again, counselor, you may post the bail by signature for Miss Taylor and she can be released immediately."

"Thank you, your honor," Darcie said.

The judge stood up, and everyone else did. He stepped down from the bench and made his exit out the back door.

"Damn you're good," DeMax said.

The bailiff removed the handcuffs from Shelly and walked over to Darcie.

"Get her bail posted and we'll release her," he said. "She can remain in the courtroom until you do."

"Thanks," Darcie said. "Mecana, you and DeMax hang out with her. I'll get her clothes and post the bail."

"Alright," Mecana said. "Shelly, come sit with us until she gets back."

Shelly walked over to Mecana and DeMax and sat down.

"Thank you," she said. "Will Darcie represent me?"

"I don't know," Mecana said. "That's Darcie's call."

"I thought of something I didn't tell you before," she said.

"What?"

"There was a new-looking black Cadillac Escalade parked in the alley behind us when me and Tanner went out the exit door."

"Anyone in it?"

"No," Shelly said. "I didn't pay much attention to it at the time. Don't remember any of the plate numbers, but I had seen it parked there before. Tanner always parked in the alley and we went out the exit door when he would get me out of jail."

"Kind of stupid to steal cocaine from a police station," DeMax said.

"I tried to talk him out of it," Shelly said. "He knew the drugs belonged to Mario and was going to show his brother how smart he was. What he didn't know was the cocaine was being held as evidence against Mario. And with no evidence, his lawyer got him off."

"His lawyer named Hayes?" Mecana asked.

"I don't know," Shelly said.

"You know who arrested Mario for the drugs?"

"A black dude named Blount. He's arrested me twice, too."

Mecana and DeMax looked at each other. "We'll pay him a visit," Mecana said.

Darcie walked back in with a piece of paper in her hand and Shelly's bag of clothes in the other.

"Okay, you're free to go when you sign the bail contract. There's a clause that makes you responsible for good behavior and to report every Friday here for visual contact. That means if you go back to prostitution they will revoke your bail and put you back in jail." Darcie handed Shelly a pen to sign the bail contract and she signed it.

"Will you represent me?" Shelly asked.

"I'll think about for a couple weeks, see how you're doing," Darcie said.

"I'll change, I promise."

"We'll talk later, go put your clothes on. Mecana and DeMax will take you home. I'll deliver your bail contract to the bailiff."

Shelly hugged Darcie's neck, then Mecana and DeMax. "Thank you." She took her clothes and headed for the restroom.

"You were great as usual," Mecana said, looking at Darcie.

DeMax nodded in agreement.

"Thanks," she said. "Now, Mecana, if you'll take DeMax and Shelly home, I'll meet you back at the house."

Shelly walked out of the restroom, dressed.

"I'll take you home Shelly," Mecana said.

"Behave yourself, Shelly," Darcie said and smiled.

Chapter 26

As Mecana dropped off Shelly, her little girl came running out the door. Shelly picked her up and carried her in the trailer.

"Everyone should have a second chance," DeMax said.

"She will," Mecana said. "Let's swing by the police station and see if Blount's there. He may tell us something useful he doesn't know he's doing."

"Would have to be that way. Don't think he would if he knew it was to our benefit," DeMax said. "I'll call Mabre and let her know it will be a while until I get home."

"She working?" Mecana asked.

"No, she's home," DeMax said. "She starts her new network job next week. She won't have to wait tables anymore. We're thinking about getting us a house after we both get some money put away."

"That's a good idea," Mecana said.

He parked in the alley behind the homicide department next to a no parking sign. The dumpster was no more than ten feet from the property exit door. The alley was wide enough for the big garbage trucks to drive through. They got out and opened the dumpster door. It was heavy so it wouldn't blow open. It had miscellaneous trash in the dumpster. Nothing that looked like it would have come from the homicide department. They got back in the truck and Mecana drove to the pay parking lot in front of the building, parked, got a ticket and made their way up to the homicide department on the fourth floor, looking for Blount.

When Mecana and DeMax walked in, the only detectives were Blount, Chandler and tailor-dressed Bennie Modele.

Chandler saw them walk in and stared at them as they walked over to Blount's desk.

"What are you doing here, Mecana?" Chandler said. "Walt's talking to the police chief about that maniac killer you and Sunday can't seem to catch."

"Wanted to ask Blount about the arrest of Mario Rosano," Mecana said.

Blount leaned back in his chair. "What for?"

"Found out the drugs Tanner stole from the property room caused you to lose your Rosano case. May be some connection with Tanner stealing the drugs."

"His attorney was behind Tanner stealing the cocaine so we wouldn't have any evidence," Blount said.

"What makes you so sure of that," Mecana said.

"He even had the nerve to come by that day and ask us to cut a deal with the prosecution before we knew the drugs were stolen," Chandler said.

"Was that Hayes?"

"Yeah, must be one of your friends. Should be disbarred," Chandler said.

"You know what kind of car Hayes has and where he parked that day?"

"Take your misguided brother with you and leave us alone," Blount said.

"You keep DeMax out of this."

"Yeah, I may have to sic Darcie on you," DeMax said and grinned.

"I don't remember," Blount said.

"Chandler, you're a stickler for records and procedure," Mecana said.

"I could look it up but I won't."

Chandler looked at Blount and waved his head toward the door and they got up and walked out.

Mecana walked over to Bennie Modele's desk.

Modele was looking good after recuperating from the wounds he got helping Mecana protect Candy Kane from assassins. He was wearing one of his tailored suits with his usual sour-puss expression.

"I guess you were listening, Bennie," Mecana said.

"Didn't have a choice. I have to be on their side. You don't work here anymore, remember."

"You ever see Attorney Hayes here?"

"Don't get me involved in this, Mecana."

"Who saved your ass when you were shot?"

"You and Darcie," he said.

"How about returning the favor then."

Bennie shook his head and gave Mecana one of his signature frowns. "A few times as I remember." he said. "He was always in a hurry like he had ants in his pants and would leave from the property room exit door to save time and money in the parking lot."

"Have you mentioned this to Walt or Sunday?"

"No, why should I?"

"One more favor, Bennie, and we'll go away," Mecana said. "Pull up Gipson Hayes and see what kind of vehicle he drives. Give me the license number and his home address."

Modele turned to his computer and ran the check.

"Only one Gipson Hayes in the system. Has a 2018 black Cadillac Escalade. Plate TYB1028. Address is 23745 Terrence Heights, Dallas. Here, I'll write it down for you so you won't come back." He picked up a pen and notepad and wrote the information down and handed it to Mecana. "He works for Berman," Bennie said.

"Thanks," Mecana said.

Mecana and DeMax walked out to the parking lot and paid the tab. Mecana started his truck and checked the addresses on his navigation system.

"Are you thinking what I'm thinking?" DeMax said.

"Yeah. He may be the one who picked up the bag but not the killer. We have to keep an open mind," Mecana said. "No evidence, but a chance a comment might tell us a lot. I'll call Sunday. According to the agreement we made with Walt we can't arrest him. We need someone who can. I've got goosebumps just thinking about it."

"Me too," DeMax said. "You just can't see them as well."

"We'll check Berman's law firm first," Mecana said.

Mecana drove to Berman Associates law firm. It was after five so the office was closed.

"Glad we didn't call Sunday," Mecana said. "Would have been going to the wrong place."

Mecana dialed Sunday.

"We're still here," she said

"Found out the attorney, Gipson Hayes, used the property room exit when he came to the station on the day Tanner stole the box. I got the description of his vehicle and it matches what Shelly saw in the alley on that day. I need your help in case he's the one we're looking for. The law firm is closed. I have his home address, though."

"Holy shit, I would have never believed it," Sunday said.

"It might not be him but we have enough to follow it up," Mecana said.

"You don't have enough for me to call a SWAT team but me and Eddy will meet you as soon as we can get there. I'll have two cruisers accompany us and have them block off the street."

"The address is 23745 Terrence Heights in Dallas. We'll meet you on the corner before we go in."

"We have to go in first," Sunday said. "Don't want it thrown out in court for violating his rights."

"Sometimes it's better not to let people know what you're doing," DeMax said.

"Okay," Mecana said. "We'll back you up."

"We're on our way," Sunday said.

Chapter 27

When Mecana pulled up to stop on the corner to wait for Sunday and Eddy, Gipson's house was in view. The garage door was closed. No way to know if he was home.

"You bring your weapon?" Mecana asked DeMax.

"I forgot it," he said.

"Sounds like shades of Mexico again. There's one in the glove box."

DeMax opened the glove box and took out a nine-millimeter pistol. He pulled the slide and pushed the safety off.

Mecana drew his Glock from his shoulder holster.

A black and white drove up behind them. Eddy and Sunday got out and drew their weapons and walked up to Mecana's truck.

"Have you seen him?" Eddy asked.

"Not yet. The garage was closed when we got here and we haven't seen any movement in the house since," Mecana said.

"Mecana, you and DeMax move around to the back," Sunday said. "I'll have cruisers block the street and the rest can join us in front and back. Don't shoot unless he's got a gun pointed at you."

Mecana and DeMax nodded. Sunday motioned for them to approach the house.

She walked up on the front porch to the front door and rang the doorbell, stepping to the side of the door. Eddy and the other cop took a prone position aiming at the house. No one came to the door. Sunday rang the door bell again. Nothing. Sunday motioned towards the door and Eddy jumped up, ran to the door and kicked it open with a high martial arts kick. He rolled into the house and came up holding his weapon, ready to fire. Sunday and the cop followed him in. Eddy made his way to the back door and opened it.

Mecana, DeMax and the cop came in with weapons drawn. They all eased through the house, checking every room, DeMax checking the garage. No cars. A yellow cat came running by, scaring the hell out of them and ran out the open back door.

Mecana entered a bedroom with a busted computer monitor on the floor. One wall was covered with law books and horror novels. An O. Henry short story collection caught Mecana's eye. He took it off the shelf and showed it to Sunday.

"He knew," Mecana said and dropped the book on the bed.

"Yeah," Sunday said. "But where the hell is he?"

One of the cops yelled from the bathroom and they all charged in.

Mecana spotted the Gladstone bag on the floor right way with an open phone book sitting on top.

A makeup box was sitting on the sink, with one of the little drawers pulled out and a bright red lipstick tube in it. An empty wig holder was sitting beside the makeup box with several brown hairs in the sink.

They all stared at the items, trying to digest the reasons for them.

"He's disguised him self as a woman," Sunday finally said. "That accounts for the weird look from the first murder. He was disguised then, too."

Mecana picked up the open phone book off the Gladstone bag.

"Look at this," he said. "With all his things still laying out he's in a hurry to get there." He handed the phone book to Sunday. She looked at it and checked her phone for who was with which Mary Kelly and called the stakeout cops.

"Adams, are you and Waxman with Mary Kelly?" Sunday asked.

"No she's working. I'm parked in the lot at the VA hospital, watching her car. Waxman is with her on the fourth floor."

"Leave the parking lot, go to her and tell Waxman we think the killer may be on his way there disguised as a woman. Tell the nurses to move their patients to another floor and stay away from the fourth floor until we tell them it's clear. You and Waxman get Mary Kelly to the ground floor and we should be there by then. Do it now." Sunday put her phone away.

"She's working at the Veterans hospital on the fourth floor. Let's go," Sunday said. "I'll call a SWAT team to meet us there."

Everyone ran out of the house, jumped in their vehicles and headed for the hospital.

Across town, Gipson drove into the VA parking lot. He got out wearing his brown wig, makeup, blue dress and high heels. His legs covered with skin-colored hose, carrying a purse with the Ripper's knife inside. He walked to the elevator and went up to the fourth floor, got off and sat down in the waiting room watching the activities to get acquainted with procedures and to pick out his victim. All the employees had name tags.

A nurse with brown hair and eyes was walking down the hallway toward him, escorted by two officers. She had 'Mary Kelly' on her name tag. They knew he was here. He picked up his purse and went to the ladies room across the hall.

Sunday, Mecana and the cops drove up to the hospital entrance and got out.

"Smith, you and Downs stop anyone from coming in or going out and move them away from the doors," Sunday said. "We're going to the fourth floor. Tell Knowles when the SWAT team arrives to let hospital security know what's happening and secure all the ground floor exits."

"I got it," he said.

Gipson was sitting on the commode when he heard the door open and someone walk in. A mans voice yelled, "Anyone in here?"

Gipson raised his feet up and removed the knife from the purse and waited. He heard massive footsteps outside the restroom. The door closed and he left the stall and peeked out the door.

He saw nurses and aides pushing beds to the elevator, then Sunday and her crew stepped off an elevator. A nurse was running toward the restroom and darted inside. He turned away and she ran to an open stall. He opened the stall door and swung the Ripper knife, cutting her throat. He jerked her name tag off her scrubs as she fell against the stall wall, blood running down her clothes over her panties to the floor. He left his purse on the floor and put the knife inside his dress.

When Gipson saw a bed coming toward him in the hall, he opened the restroom door and grabbed the bed, helping push it to an elevator. Cops were checking everyone getting on the elevator. When he got to the elevator, he let go and another nurse was holding it, waiting to get on the elevator. He moved backwards slowly to the stairwell and opened the exit door. When no one saw him, he walked down one flight of stairs and got off with his new name tag on and walked down the hall in a hurry to an elevator no cops were checking. He got on the elevator and punched the button for the basement floor.

The elevator made a stop on every floor, but no one checked him with his name tag on. He looked like any of the other overweight middle-aged nurses.

SWAT team leader Roy Knowles got a call from Sunday.

"He's not on the fourth floor. Block all the exits," she said. "He knows we're on to him. He didn't get Kelly but he cut a nurse's throat."

Gipson got off the elevator on the basement floor and two cops were standing in front of him. He jerked the nearest one to him, stabbed him in the back, then dropped the knife and grabbed his gun. He mowed down the other cop with several rounds and ran out the outside door carrying the cop's M15 pistol.

He ran across the lawn and was spotted by members of the SWAT team who opened fire at him. He returned fire and they ducked down behind their cars. H kicked his high heels off and jumped over a fence, still wearing the dress, and climbed in his car. Bullets were ripping holes in the side of his car, missing the tires. He floor-boarded the Caddy's gas pedal, at least ten cop cars and Mecana following. Ten miles down the road, he made a quick turn through a neighborhood and they lost him.

"Where the hell is he going?" DeMax said.

Mecana put the pedal to the metal and called Darcie. "I'm in a chase with Hayes now, he's definitely the one."

"Oh no," she said. "You take too many chances, Mecana. You're going to make me a widow.

"Just too much at stake."

"I know. You never give up for the right reasons."

"See if he has a childhood address."

"Just a minute," she said. "Home town address was 421 Old Farrow Road in Reesville."

Mecana made a u-turn and hit the interstate, going west towards Reesville.

Five miles down the road, DeMax spotted Gipson.

"There he is," DeMax said.

Mecana followed as Gipson weaved around a truck.

"He's got a lot more power than I have," Mecana said. "I'll let him run and meet him there."

In minutes, a city limits sign appeared. Reesville, Texas – Population 2219, it read.

Mecana called Sunday. "I have him in sight. He's going to his old home address: 421 Old Farrow Road in Reesville."

"Okay," Sunday said. "We're on our way now. How do you know?"

"There's nothing else left for him," Mecana said. "He knows that."

Gipson turned off the exit and drove down to a side road to his old two-story house. He stopped at the gate, revving the motor like he was getting ready for a big race, Mecana getting closer.

Gipson punched the Caddy, tore down the fence and crashed through the front of the house into the front room, walls caving in on him. The fuel tank on the Cadillac exploded.

Flames shot up to the ceiling and within seconds he was trapped inside his car. Ceiling fire debris covered the Caddy. The house and car were burning like a college bonfire. The chase was over.

Mecana picked up his phone and dialed. "Sunday, you can slow down. He's burning alive, too late to get him out."

"How did that happen?" she asked.

"He crashed into the house. The gas tank exploded."

"We'll be there in about ten minutes. You can probably hear us now."

"Yep, I hear you," Mecana said and hung up.

"What are we going to do after this is over?" DeMax asked.

Mecana grinned. "You assume you're my partner whatever it is, huh?"

"How about we open a restaurant like Simon did. We could get killed doing this."

"Too hard of work for me," Mecana said, looking in his rearview mirror. "I see Sunday coming in with a herd. I bet there are twenty cars behind her."

"Good," DeMax said. "Mabre didn't want me to come but I knew I had to. I'm your partner, it's what I do."

"Thanks, DeMax," Mecana said. "After Sunday gets here we'll go home and think about what to do next."

"Sounds like a good idea to me," DeMax said.

Darcie was waiting at the front door when Mecana drove in after taking DeMax home. When he got out of his truck, she ran to him, hugged his neck and kissed him.

"Talk about a warm welcome," he said.

"I was very worried about you chasing that monster," Darcie said.

"We caught him more by accident than evidence. He killed himself, burned to death in his Cadillac. With his DNA, I would think several other cases will be solved. Shelly remembering the Cadillac is what made this all happen."

"Thank god it's over. Time to move on now."

"I've been thinking about that," Mecana said. "If our families can't come to see us we go to see them. We take some time off, think about what we want to do next and include DeMax and Mabre."

"They are like family now," Darcie said.

"I could spend some time with my kids, take you to Waco to see your family. You and Marcie could dress alike and see if I can tell identical twins apart. We may have a wedding to go to soon. Eddy's going to propose to Sunday."

"She knows. She's going to say yes."

"What I thought. I have some other things in mind, too."

"You always do."

Mecana took off his jacket and sat it on a chair on the porch. He unbuttoned his shirt and threw it on top of the jacket.

"What are you doing?" Darcie asked.

"Thinking about what else I want to do." He picked up Darcie and walked through the open door, kicked it closed with his foot and carried her to the bathroom.

Darcie rubbed her hand across Mecana's bare chest.

"You're a mind reader," he said.

"No, but I know you."

"I wouldn't want to be anyone else."

THE END

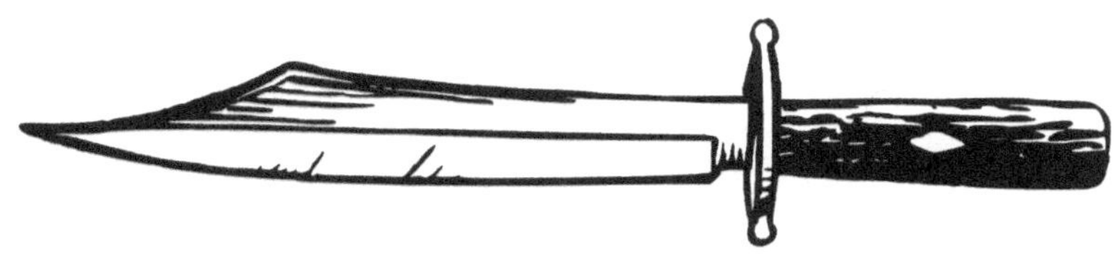

LIFE GOES ON

About the Author

John L. Lansdale was born and raised in East Texas. He is married to the love of his life Mary. They have four children. He is a retired Army reserve Psychological Operations Officer and a combat veteran with numerous medals and awards. Past roles include inventor, country music songwriter and performer, and television programmer. He produced and directed the Television Special "Ladies of Country Music." He has also produced several albums in Nashville, hosted his own radio shows and won awards for producing and writing radio and television commercials.

John was also a writer and editor for a business newspaper. He has worked as a comic book writer for Tales from the Crypt, IDW, Grave Tales, Cemetery Dance and several more. He co-authored the Shadows West and Hell's Bounty novels with his brother Joe R. Lansdale. He is also the author of Zombie Gold, Horse of a Different Color, Slow Bullet, When the Night Bird Sings, Broken Moon, The Last Good Day, Long Walk Home and several other titles.

TITLES from JOHN L. LANSDALE

SLOW BULLET
Army veteran Clark McKay is searching for the truth behind his best friend's murder. This search takes him across the globe, where he meets a multitude of characters and is forced to wade through the murky Washington DC waters of corruption. Clark McKay wants to find a murderer... but what happens when he uncovers so much more?

LONG WALK HOME
The O'Rourke family lives on a fading farm in the small town of Angel Point, Mississippi. With family, friends and neighbors fighting overseas in WWII - and rising racial tensions back home - the summer of 1944 turns into a nightmare of murder and loss. One boy's life changes forever after a chance encounter with someone nobody thought possible.

BOY AND HOG
In the deep woods, anything can happen. A group of white-collar workers with a hand-drawn map trek into the wilderness for a hunting expedition. But out there, will they be the hunters or the prey?

BOY AND HOG RETURN
While on patrol, two game wardens stumble onto a grisly scene hidden deep in the woods. With backup on the way, will the wardens survive the wait, or will unexpected visitors send them to an early grave?

EMERGENCY CHRISTMAS
Join the Albright family and the guest who surprises them just in time for the holiday. Along the way, they discover sometimes crisis brings a family closer together.

THE MECANA SERIES by JOHN L. LANSDALE

HORSE OF A DIFFERENT COLOR – Mecana Series #1
Dallas PD Detective Thomas Mecana is on the hunt for a serial killer terrorizing the Lone Star State. Joining him is Darcie Connors, a young officer working her first murder case. With hard work, and some luck, Mecana and his partner discover a most-unusual serial killer case with murder in its very genes.

WHEN THE NIGHT BIRD SINGS – Mecana Series #2
Detectives Thomas Mecana and Darcie Connors are on the trail of a new suspect. With an ever-growing suspect list, Mecana must toe the line between friend and foe. Each action leaves them sitting in the crosshairs of danger. One wrong move could mean the end.

TWISTED JUSTICE – Mecana Series #3
Dallas Homicide Detective Sunday Verves is looking into the suspicious deaths of local drug runners when she discovers a potential suspect that hits too close to home. When the trail leads her south of the border, she enlists some old friends to track down the suspects.

THE BOX – Mecana Series #4
Detective Thomas Mecana and the gang get back together for one last case. Mecana soon finds the case will also bring him back to where it all began. This horror-filled novel brings the Mecana Series to a close.

www.ingramcontent.com/pod-product-compliance
Lightning Source LLC
Chambersburg PA
CBHW050537190726

48284CB00003B/1113